SWINE FEVER

Y. J. J. HAN

CONTENTS

&

Poems

Ch. 1

*T*hat summer, even the storms got away. It was too hot.

On the old radio over the wall, someone's noisy sound to watch out for the daytime temperature is over 40 degrees Celsius, still remained in my ear, and I longed for the tedium of the season and the pouring rain. In this summer, I was just thinking that these monsters in front of my eyes would soon be gone, forgetting the plight of the homeless on the streets. Then how did I endure the summer?

There may be people to ask. Me? I barely survived that summer. It is not because of the heat. It seemed that they had made me want to tell me what I saw all the things in their foolish, arrogant and stubborn monsters. Do I have to thank you for the current situation? I do not even think about it. It is not hot in the summer. It is not just that I cannot stand the breath of moisture and heat that pushes from the south, but the disgust of the realities above it. How deep is the heart? In addition, what is the thickness of both sides? It was hard to know. The coexistence of evil and goodness seems to exist.

I am lucky now to survive only in the two worlds that are being destroyed. It was hard to expect humility. The world that has always woken up from sleep has had to see things filled with pride and dirty desires. I was not free either. I had thought that I would rather not wake up from sleep. The hot and humid weather could not stand it. The intense sunlight has turned the whole world into dark brown. There is a saying that this earth is getting hot, but the heat like the fireball that cannot stand in the body seemed to come out through all the holes. They became one with evil spirits and gradually made them monsters. The earth is holding a hot fireball. Moreover, this fireball makes hot springs on various surfaces of the earth. Many of them raise the temperature even more. Humidity and heat seemed to make every living thing on the ground go crazy. Humidity and heat seemed to drive all living things on the ground.

Even a little stimulation of feelings leads to contention and even murder due to discomfort index. It is difficult for anyone to find the same composure before an unpleasant humidity and high temperature. Sometimes I looked up at the cloudless sky. There were many times when I waited, hoping that there would be a small cloud, or that it would bring me a shower. However, I could not even have such a wish before the horror season was over. The forest fires, which do not know where they started, have not been evolved yet. Nothing remained where the forest fire had passed. The shape of the body was horrible and the water in the valley, where I played and swam when I was young, disappeared with dark ash. Survivors had to prepare for another death as they had large and small holes in their lungs.

Life is so cruel to the living and the dead.

What is the boundary between the living and the dead? Is it a solid material that is not broken into anything or very thin ice covered the surface of the lake in the beginning of winter?

It may be something like ice that cannot be verified without actually walking on it. Many people are deceived by the reality. The boundary is ambiguous. I am breathing like this, but in reality, my reality may be deceiving others.

I am alive but in fact dead. Is to survive in the heat through this unbearable floor and to live parasitically in a different shell for a total blowout. Oblivion is truly scary. Already in my brain, any memories like a small broken piece of puzzle go around between the dull cells. It was a brutal shadow. Moreover, the shadows were brainwashed by all the ugly events of the time, and were becoming insensitive.

Sometimes I found myself in a small space trying to catch those torn puzzles in a fantasy with some paranoid symptoms. It was a terrible struggle for things to be easily forgotten, rather than to forget everything. I was hoping the harsh season would pass by. As time went on, everything on the ground began to hide one by one. There were no visitors.

Sometimes it was early to find a golden eagle on a dry branch that had taken off its leaves and watched over the barren riverbank and flew somewhere. The land was said to have long been an area of indigenous people.

Now those who will be scattered around by strange immigrants. Everywhere, the bridle of violence grows like a poisonous mushroom. It is like a bum in the woods that is hard to distinguish between edible and inedible. There are as many excuses for violence as there are numbers spread.

One by one, the boundaries of the goodness collapse.
I do not know where to start the story. The beginning of this story is just a horror, but fragments of memory that are

somewhat impractical will have to be fitted first. Its share is of the readers. However, all I have to do is to always be alert.

Moreover, you have to know who I am. If you have at least a sense of which you are and if you can see the reality right in any situation, you can avoid the danger. Everyone knows that this simple and common sense should not escape, but the hardest thing is to put it into practice.

A lake with thin ice is dangerous. However, people are easily deceived by this obvious fact. Curiosity is a shortcut that can sometimes be the most dangerous. Curiosity and greed are the fastest roads to destruction. They argue over who is better and superior talent, and use all the means and methods to prove it. The most dangerous trap is right inside. The exact location of the interior is unknown but does not give up until the target falls down with grasping the weak point. The most powerful and irrevocable enemy lies within us. Therefore, we are deceived. Sometimes light pride comes to risk. We must always find a way to survive.

In the jungle, you should always keep the tension. When the senses are blunt or the judgment is blurred, they are in danger because they cannot easily grasp the situation.

The hot weather makes people's senses obscure. It does not distinguish boundaries. It is easy to stand in the wrong direction to choose which one. Sometimes I see animals herd in the wild. The role of the chief among them is important.

The chief cannot always lead the crowd to a safe place because he can make mistakes. You can see many tragedies once you make a wrong choice. The thing that can judge the situation is to get wisdom about reality. We must learn from everything around us. The rainbow reminds me of a lesson in the flood. The volcano reminds us of the judgment of fire. Some of them become teachers for us.

We must lower ourselves. You always have to find a low seat in a feast. It is then possible to grasp the situation of all reality properly. Look at the greedier scene you see. It is a foolish thing that soon does not even realize the danger that will come before them. It was once a peaceful place.

It would have been the quietest place and the surrounding area full of satisfying oneself. It would have been a place to eat and enjoy peace and abundance while eating the daily food for the day. The fields are filled with things to eat, and sometimes the rain that falls from the sky is wet in the earth. I remember where it was beautiful. Everyone will be eager to return to that time.

Nevertheless, I have already passed through a long time tunnel. Our place has already been ruined and there is no space left to return. Only the stars in the night sky looked at the long trail of a meteor falling to the ground from time to time. In some memories, there will be hidden pieces. Now it is buried, but someday the fragments of that memory will rise again, knocking on the surface of thought.

The memories of the seasons of the days, when the dead sculptures of the fallen ones, will rise one by one. Leafy leaves that have fallen to the ground in advance due to heavy rains that have prompted the fall and winter are still in a pale blue light. It may be due to the moisture coming from deep in the ground. I saw that it was living without dying and enduring a severe drought.

If anyone had shared their terrible vitality at all, they would have enjoyed the joy of surviving on this path together. Everything was chaotic at the time. Like steam coming out of the ground everywhere, it happened without warning.

The damp energy brought the madness to life from the gloom and instinct. They were colorful pigs that ate all sorts of small things and parasitic little beasts, eating their droppings.

The stench and rotten smells of food were everywhere. Sometimes I went out to the river to get rid of this disgusting smell. From Jackson to the Mississippi River I could reach half a day. The long stretches of the red river show a sublime cleansing from the inside. The surrounding cotton fields participate in a pure ritual, displaying white flesh as if to express the pilgrims' hearts. No breath is heard on the street. Silence was often viewed as a plan for fears and pressing worries about the future. That river probably will not begin or end. Many living things would have been dying here. Maybe I was still practicing hard about the end of my life.

The body cannot stink all the time until it dies, with the umbilical cord attached to its mother's belly. Until the young juniper trees grow up and become big branches and oxidize themselves with axes. Nothing can escape evil instincts. I do not reject any noble sacrifice to hide the ugly side.

Ch. 2

*I*t was about the end of the hot summer.

The end of the wind blowing from where the sun still shines was a warm aura. A small disturbance arose. Anyone could hear a common sound.

"Look, all night, somebody has dug under the stone wall! And put everything here, damn, look at these crap, I think it's nauseous." The sound was from a pig, which had a red fur, Jack. He is the most influential here.

Despite his unfamiliar pronunciation, there were many who followed him. It was huge, and its lips were torn from side to side, covering the half of the face. He was always the one who made the tension of this place.

"Look at this, Jack; you should not let it go. If you do not catch the thief right away, you'll have more damage." It was Jim who hanging out with Jack. His body size was not even half of Jack, but his fur was also red. They were always together, thinking and behaving as if they were part of the same family.

"Jim, you cannot set a sentry every night, though, of course, there are a lot of guys living around us, but not all of us! We cannot afford to lose our time, and we should sleep at night."

"Jack, I still do not understand what I mean, so keep in

mind that this opportunity is a time to make more of our troops." Jack thought about his words for a while.

Jim is better than me to think for sure. When we looked around, we knew that the number of followers was small. In this spacious space, there are many other pigs as well as Jack and Jim. They all had different fur color, but they were pigs, and in the middle, there were mixed animals.

The total number was about 100.

I thought it was too narrow for anyone to see. In this narrow space, you are guaranteed a comfortable life, depending on who takes the lead in life. Jack and Jim have become one in this regard, deep in their hearts. The combination of Jack's strength and Jim's cunningness seemed to be able to climb up to the power of those groups at once.

It is impossible to take control of a group of about 100 by force. It needed a tricky plan like a snake. I thought Jim was the kind of co-worker that helped me.

"Jim, what should we do, we cannot beat them with just one of us. We are being treated entirely out of the world here. Look at this. We are treated like strangers here, fucking eyes, all on the lookout for those eyes." Many guys wanted to get attention from any group. Jack and Jim were also among the crowd that wanted to be the head of the group.

However, the reality was not so bright. No one had ever seriously considered his or her presence.

Sometimes it is easy to be caught up in the cover, knowing that the intensities that you want to be a top can sometimes give you a serious defeat.

"Jack! Do not worry about, I have an idea,"

he said, "We can't just stand around like this forever. Do you remember when we first came here?"

"Then don't forget, then you and I came here together. Then you and I came here together, when you and I were very young ... I do not even know where this place is, it's treated like a nuisance like a bum on the ground ... How could you forget that time? Now our situation is too shabby." Whenever we were here, we thought of a pleasant revolt.

It is like our revolution that has not come true yet.

This revolution is bound to cost someone. With the utmost selfishness to hope that, we were not included in the sacrifice.

Just because we do not practice does not mean we are a coward. We just spent our time planning everything and preparing the things we needed. We loathe calling this an excuse for cowardice. We needed a sympathizer to join us in our revolution. Jim and Jack together had a late lunch and promised to meet again under the oak tree in the backyard. Lunch was all about dried peas and a few potatoes that had a bad smell that did not know where they came from. Some of them bossed me around, intercepted the line, and took away all the few left. Indeed, the life here was boring. We needed a groundbreaking opportunity to overturn something.

It was terribly hot today. It was so hot that I felt confused. For a few days, it really was like peeling the soles of the feet as if the ground had heated the frying pan. First, I ate lunch quickly and ran to the place I was supposed to meet. Jim was already there waiting for me under the shade of a tree.

"Look, Jim! It's boiling today."

"Jack! Come on. The shade of this tree cools the sweat off."

"Curse it! On such a hot day, I have to eat some meat, but every day, I started to feel dizzy from a few days ago, because I had a few rotten potatoes."

Jack spoke as he climbed the hill gasping for breath.

"You're right, Jack, and we're going to die of malnutrition."

"Jim, don't you have any good ideas? We have been friends for a long time. It's time for you to have a good idea."

"Well, Jack, I think it's first time to get rid of those who oppose us."

"Our opponents? You're talking about someone who doesn't like us?"

"Right, Jack, there's someone standing on the other side of us in everything, so it's hard for us to do anything about it."

"Who do you think it is?"

We also opened our mouths at the same time as if we were in mutual agreement.

"He's Chuck!"

Chuck was the longest-living pig here. He is probably the oldest. His influence was not to be ignored. The wrinkles of the face were deep and long and descended to the neck, and the skin was white. He had a great ability to use his head even he was old. The creatures that live in this place talked to him about their troubles once and got counseling.

The ability to solve the problem was great. There were still many creatures under his influence. We had to be more careful to deal with it. However, if we do not get past him, he was such a threat to us that we gave up our plan.

"How can we get him out of our sight? Jim, think about it in your head! But don't you think your using idea is better between us?"

"We can't win by force, but we have to find his weakness. If we use that weak spot, he'll give up."

"Weak spot? I don't know what it is except for the fact that he is older."

"Yes, you told me the right answer. It is his age. I've seen him make mistakes because he's old."

"What mistake?"

"It seems like his memory has become weak. Well, a few days ago, I saw he couldn't even remember the food he borrowed."

"Well, a weakened memory? How do we use it?"

It was clear that Chuck's memory was in trouble when it came time. His age is now over 20 years old, and he has lived far beyond his average life expectancy. In our world, he has already lived enough. Last time I had lent him a few potatoes. He surely promised to pay back tomorrow. I have clearly heard the promise that it will be combined with interest. The next day I told him to repay the borrowed potato, but what he said was true ridiculousness itself. When he said that he had not borrowed them, I did not have any words for him.

Now, I thought this guy was crazy or got dementia. He was angry now, and once he was out of his place, telling me not to deal with him. He must have been both mentally and physically decrepit. I have seen many his mistakes. He tried to pass the mistake on to familiar humor. His gimmick also seemed so perfect that no one could notice. Nevertheless, for me, all his mistakes never slipped by. One day I approached him and said,

"Look at this, Uncle Chuck or grandpa, how am I supposed to call you? Anyway, is not your judgment and behavior the same as before? Did anything happen?"

He was astonished by my keen question, he closed his eyes thoughtfully, and staring for a moment at the big apple tree behind me. Moreover, he said,

"Jim, I've never thought I'm as old as you think I am. Look, I still judge and think, but I am as keen and accurate as a young man is. There are still a lot of followers here who follow me and respect me. Thank you for your concern anyway."

Although he said something that seemed to protect him, it was all an excuse to me. It was obvious that he was getting old. After a moment is thought, a rustling sound looked in the direction of Jack. He was chewing something out of his pocket. I quickly grabbed his hand and looked at what was in his palm. It was a dried potato peel.

"Look at this, Jack! What are you doing now? In the meantime, you are all thinking about food!"

"I'm sorry, Jim. I feel hungry because I ate less lunch. So I'm going to pick up some potatoes peel that's on the ground and try it."

"This is not the time. What did I say earlier? Say what I said once again!"

He was poking his white nostrils with a big finger, scratching his head on the other side.

"Well, what was it?"

His reaction was not so surprising. That is because I have often seen it. Isn't that stupid Jack who listens to the other person and forgets when he turns around?

"Look, Jack. I told you Chuck's old and now his memory is blurred, and he is starting to wane. We said we should take advantage of that weakness. Am I right?"

"Oh, I did. I'm sorry, Jim..."

I thought to him you stupid white pig Jack!

"Look at this, Jack, we're a red pig and very young which has only lived for ten years. Take a closer look at your skin color. What inspiration does not come up?"

"What inspiration? It just looks red all over."

The stupidly big Jack was scratching his stomach with his long claws. It was indeed pathetic.

"Jack, I feel the intensity of burning like a fireball in my mind every time I see red."

"The red color is sort of ... it might be a little exciting for some people."

"We are sort of family, we do everything hotly, and we'll work together again this time."

"I agree with you, Jim, I'll help you, please let me know if there is anything I need to do, but Jim, we feel that the number of red pigs is too small, at least 10 out of 100, but the white is about 40. I am still questioning the possibility."

"Jack, you're the problem with being so sentimental! Numbers do not matter. I don't care how much they're outnumbered by us."

"Why?" "How many of them are on Chuck's side? probably less than 20, the rest of them are just lethargic, thoughtless. There are about 20 people we have to deal with, including Chuck. Don't worry."

"Jim, you're so fearless. My legs are shaking at the mention of the moment."

"Use your head. We lose right now. It's most effective to use rumor to separate them."

"Using rumor?"

"Yes, empty rumor!"

"So you're making a lie?"

"That's right; we have to make such a lie that can send Chuck and his flock away in one fell swoop."

"Is that possible? Originally, Chuck is famous for being very clever, is he going to be deceived by all of us?"

"We have to make a very plausible statement, a real fake that everyone can admit."

"Jim, I can't do it with my head. I can do things by force, but I'm not good enough at using my head."

"Jack, don't worry, give me a little time, and we'll meet again tomorrow. Wait, do not meet here, we need another new place. Do you have any good places?"

"Well, there's a place where no one's interested. It is an old warehouse where the roof collapsed a long time ago and no one lived. It is not easy to approach even during the day. It is because of the lush grass. I will take some of them with me. I'll meet you there."

"Okay, but let's get together the red pigs who will cooperate in our work. Let's start the red revolution."

Ch. 3

*O*nce I talked to him in hastily, I could not figure out what to start with. Many thoughts came to mind on the way back. Our herd of red pigs has not settled here since ancient times. I do not know exactly how I lived here, but I have been led astray by someone else's hand, and have lived in a group of the same race as other red pigs. There seemed to lurk within us a hot passion that could not be expressed.

It was a kind of rebelliousness that we would not go under anyone and live in obedience. Perhaps because of the hot weather, the irritation mixed in and deepened my heart. I could not stand it. On my way back, I found a mud puddle made by a shower last night. I jumped in first, and then Jack ran together reflexively and enjoyed a muddy bath for a long time. It felt as if the heat had disappeared a little.

There is nothing like a mud bath to shake off the ticks and dust on our body. Jack and Jim rolled in the mud for a long time, grinning and gesticulating at each other. Moreover, when we felt tired, we fell down and fell asleep. We enjoyed the afternoon sun, muttering something in unnoticed words. Soon August will begin.

It is probably hotter and hotter than July. We would not mind, though. We have got urgent work piled up right now.

Perhaps the hottest and most exciting times are waiting for us red pigs. Horny sows will not dream of a shy revolution. We certainly remember them. The first days we came here, some red sows that night were pulled out by somebody and never came back. They probably tried to erase the memories of breeding. However, we cannot sit back again.

Our revolution will be complete when we dye this place with more and more dark red. However, the things that have to be overshadowed are those who are camouflaged in the fearful white color. The most intense will finally win. I imagine all things in the mud. Then we came down together from the mud garden. It was late in the evening when we returned to the residence. The dinner had already ended and was washing the dishes. Jack and I ran to the kitchen. There was Sally, a middle-aged black sow. at the end of the session; she was drinking a light cup of tea with other colleagues.

"Sally! Is dinner over already? I'm sorry it's late, but didn't you leave something to eat?" Sally screamed at us in a brusque voice.

"Look, Jack and Jim, what did I say before? Remember. If you are late for dinner, you will have nothing to eat. You think I have multiple hands?"

"Oh, Sally, don't do this. I have not eaten all day, and at best, a few potatoes in the day were all that was, what the hell are you doing here? You fucking lady!"

"What? This old and a bitchy pig Jack! What did you just say! You'll die in my hands once."

Suddenly she got up and walked up to the kitchen. It was the moment to pick something up and to strike with it. The situation seemed to be getting worse. I had to appease everyone here.

I quickly split between the two. It was not enough for me to divide the two by force because of the huge size of Sally, but I had to stop the fight. Sally's heavy punch suddenly flew into my cheek. She tried to hit Jack, but she got hit me in the middle instead.

"It hurts. Sally, did you just hit me?"

"Jim, what did I say? Didn't I tell you not to stop me? Why are you two getting hurt? Do not blame it on me. It's your fault you stepped in the middle."

Jack ducked back again, then suddenly ran up in front of me and tried to hit Sally.

"Bitch, Sally! What is wrong with the food we want? I usually do that because you ignore our red pigs. Am I wrong?"

"Look at this pig, you fucking lie. When did I ignore you red pigs?"

"Sally, the rumor's already spread out among us. Everyone knows you black pigs treated us with contempt from the start."

Sally suddenly began to tremble at Jack's words. Perhaps it was a common reaction when the truth was revealed. Jack's words made no excuse for her. Just unable to control the rising anger suddenly picked up the cup on the table and threw it at the wall.

As soon as the cup hit the wall, it smashed into pieces.

"Shit, you red pigs, if I don't see them here, I'll have a little longer life."

"You told my word, I don't feel comfortable seeing you either."

"Jack, let's stop now. It is no good for us to fight anymore. You'd better back off like this."

Jim grabbed Jack by the shoulder and blocked his next move. This seemed to be the best way to end the fight.

Sally, too, was unable to contain her anger, and, breathing heavily, stepped back and turned against us. Suddenly her black and huge back blocked our view. It was a huge body indeed. Sally's fist was also not a woman's short and weak fist. She had a powerful punch to knock down any guys with one blow. If there was a big fight between the two, Jack would have suffered a considerable wound.

"Jim, I really don't want to back off like this, but what should I do? I really cannot control an angry feeling. Give me something in my hand. I will say it is a powder keg. I'm going to have to take it easy."

I looked around for things I could give him as he requested. Something caught my eye.

It just finished cleaning and saw a broom that was not dry. I thought I should try it. As soon as Jack got it, he broke it with his knee and made it two pieces. Moreover, threw it at the wall.

"Damn, this stifling space, I have to leave this place soon, or I'll die of the disease."

When Sally saw it, she slipped back into the kitchen in a slightly wobbly attitude. It was then. The sound of the door opening was heard from behind. Chuck and his flock. His legs seemed uncomfortable, and his staff was in his hand.

They came in together, supporting Chuck.

"What the hell is this fuss about? What happened here?" The atmosphere in the room suddenly subsided heavily with Chuck's appearance. It is as if a low pressure is passing by. He was such a presence here. He had created the absolute authority for himself. Although he was ill, he still seemed to have influence. It is almost time to eat dinner and fall asleep, but now that it is here.

"It's nothing, Chuck. It's just a little ruckus."

"A little ruckus? I heard it outside, and I thought it was a big fight with Sally." Then sly Panky, which was in the crowd, suddenly interrupted and began to talk. Panky is the only hunting dog here. He was a nimble, cunning fellow. He is always been by Chuck's side, craving profits. I do not know where it came from, but Panky was the one who played the role of a watchman here.

"Hey, my name's Panky! I have survived so far without dying. I am not like you guys. Our old ancestors came from the wild. Moreover, I have a good sense of smell and hearing.

In addition, be brave. I am very good at dealing with situations. I have ears and eyes. I heard it outside, and I think it was a big fight, and that's why I brought Chuck all the way here."

"Panky, I don't think it's your business here, it's mine and Sally's. And can't you see I'm trying to put up with this?"

Chuck was listening with his eyes closed for a moment to hear the coming and going conversation between the two. Then suddenly he hit the table and started shouting loudly. I could not figure out why he was doing that.

"Everybody, Be quiet. It's really loud."

Panky, trying to split the two, looked hateful. He has never stood to defend us.

"Boss, Chuck, you can't let this happen. I think this group has lost its rank these days. The boss here is Chuck. However, Jack and Jim pretending to be right here, who are self-proclaimed leaders among these red pigs, are sure to defy order here and start a rebellion at any time. Chuck, we have to get these two guys out of here right now. That way, I think we will be in peace here. Am I right?"

"Panky, what are you talking about? What did we do anything wrong? It's just that we're hungry and we're just asking if there's anything to eat for dinner."

"Who said it was wrong? If Sally said she had nothing to eat, you should have backed away. Why would you want to make the atmosphere ugly and fight it? After all, it is both your fault! Chuck, I need you to conclude for us. What should I do? I'll gather opinions by deporting these two right now."

"Why should we leave here? This place does not belong to anyone. Panky, did you know that you're setting fire to each other's conflicts?"

"Am I creating conflict? It is bulshit! In fact, I haven't had any peaceful day since you red pigs came in here."

"Panky, that's absurd. You keep ignoring our red pigs, so we cannot just stand by and defend ourselves. Say something, Chuck! You said you were the captain here?"

Chuck heard it and said nothing for a moment. It was very different from his reaction, which he shouted as if he would do anything right away. He was just staring at the white wall. Apparently, he looked so different from before. As if, he had just forgotten his behavior.

"Chuck, Chuck, are you listening to me?"

For a while, he was gazing at the stars in the night sky through the perforated holes in the ceiling. The ceiling looked as if it would soon collapse in the rain. As if Chuck were worried about it, he just stood mute.

"What's wrong with you today, Chuck? It is so different from before! Could you give some feedback on this situation?"

"What? What did you say?"

"Don't you understand what's going on here? We need to get these red pigs out of here right now. On the other hand, we are going to mess up our lives. You have to make some kind of decision. We are waiting for your answer."

"Oh, that's it. I've been forgetting for a moment"

"Boss, why do you keep showing us this? If you do not make sure you are in order, it will be a mess all over. These Reds communists are already trying to get on top of us as they revolutionize."

Panky tried to persuade Chuck very logically. Jack listened to him and said aloud, suddenly he could not control his emotions. Perhaps Panky's expression of Communist-like men mixed with anger.

"What did you say? You said we are like the Communist Party. Are you saying through your mouth? Why are we the Communist Party?"

"Yes, I said you are a Communist. I know what you guys have in mind, and I know when you red pigs are going to come together and riot and turn this place into your world. That is exactly what the Communist Party is doing. Am I wrong?"

"That expression doesn't suit us at all. You have just spoken well. The Communist Party is not us, but you. Does this belong to you? You mean you are the owners of this place. This place is not yours. It is the place for all of us. But you white pigs behave like you're owners and very arrogant, just as if we were slaves."

Among the red swarms was a sow named Kara. It was always silent and quiet, but sometimes it served as a kind of mentor that gave us strength by making the right sound. Even though she is old, she advised us whenever we were in a crisis and taught us how to avoid problems. Kara was also listening to our conversation from beginning to end. Then suddenly she opened her mouth and began to defend us.

"You have to listen to what we're saying. I do not think our red pigs are wrong. Since we have been here, we have lived by reading your faces of white pigs, which make up the absolute majority of this group. There is nothing wrong with what we are saying now. Things would not have gotten this seriously bad if you guys were a little modest and treated us well. We do not intend to leave, and we will not. But we have an idea if we continue to get this unfair treatment."

"What's the idea?" Suddenly Sally, who was listening to a conversation from the kitchen side, was tossing out asking.

"Our thoughts?"

"Yes, I mean your thoughts. This is not just you guys. Keep in mind that we have black pigs, too. We have as many

numbers as you. We have a lot to say. But I've been patient."
Sally was a black sow. There are also many groups of black
pigs here. Perhaps as many as the number of red pigs. Is this
all? There were some pigs whose fur color was a little yellow,
even though they did not know where they came from. We
referred to them as brown strangers.

"Look at our black pigs. It is terrible. Did we come here
voluntarily? Not at all. Originally, we lived freely in a wide
field. Then one damn day, we were forced to move here. We
have not been properly treated here either. We made a
unilateral sacrifice to fill your belly. I do not like you guys. I
mean, we want to get out of this boring place if we have a
chance."

"Sally, calm down. You guys are indispensable here. If you
were not here, this place would probably have been the
dirtiest place. This place is getting organized because of you.
No one thinks you are a nuisance." Suddenly Mr. Dali, a
brown stranger who was listening quietly in a corner,
interrupted in the middle of the conversation and spoke. He
was a middle-aged male. He had a suitable body and a long
chin beard that was not suitable for his face.

Sometimes when one of our groups needs advice or a
proper judgment, he always tried to lead a conversation by
stroking his chin like a habit.

"I'm telling you, I think we all need each other. I do not
think anyone should be treated unfairly. In fact, it is
undeniable that the white pigs are leading the way. No one
has ever tried to stop or fix it. However, let us suppose it
happens. Maybe we will all disappear from here all at once.

No one wants to do that. I do not want to either. But I think there's a need to fix it."

"I don't understand what you're talking about, Mr. Dali." Panky continued to speak again. "Mr. Dali, of course I know you're being treated like a stranger here. However, you can think of it like this. Not all of us are from home. I just do not know why I am here. Somehow, we got ourselves here, and we got a bunch of people who did not want to see each other. However, don't we need a strict order here, too? If we just let it live, it will be a mess. I am not letting anyone destroy this order. I spoke on behalf of our boss, Chuck."

"Panky, Chuck's still there, but why do you stand up and make order, I think you're rather destroying this order, but I hope you'll if you keep quiet, we'll be able to find peace again after this conflict ends!"

Jim looked at Panky again and said, he seemed to be trying to end the fight here. He does not think the conversation will help them.

Chuck, who had been listening to all the conversation, slowly began to open his heavy mouth. Everyone stared at his wide, big lips.

"Well, I mean, the conversation you've had, I've heard so well...but what? What was it about?"

"What are you talking about, Chuck? Do you know who I am? I am the one who is always around you. Your errand boy and spokesman!"

"Yeah, that's right. You are Panky! I am sorry. I have had a short lapse. But what did we talk about?"

"Oh, what are you talking about? Now, Chuck, these red

piglets are challenging our authority, and we have told you to kick them out of here right away. Do you know what I'm talking about now?"

"That's right, I said that, and I was angry because I could not bear it. During the conversation, several pigs interjected and it seemed that I had forgotten me for a while. god damn it!"

Apparently, there was an unusual signal for Chuck's health. It was not that arrogant and forced look of the past.

I decided to wait and see what he would say for a moment.

"Look at these; I'll say something to you as the boss here. I hate it the most because it was not like that in the old days. When I saw the noise and the argument, I came out and cleaned up. However, not now. I do not want to interfere in anything. I want to live a little quietly. However, I have been keeping an eye on you red pigs' behavior. I wonder what you guys are thinking. I admit I am not what I used to be. However, that does not change the order here. I will speak respectfully on behalf of this place. You red pigs had better leave this place. However, not right now. I will give you one more chance. The opportunity is to get you guys out of here tomorrow morning to get food for us. This will continue until when the anger subsides and order is established. Do you understand?"

"What did you say?"

I doubted my ears as soon as he finished speaking. Maybe I heard the wrong thing. At the thought of doing, I saw Jack's face beside me. He stood still, frozen in the spot, unable to say anything in a daze.

I could not say this without Chuck going mad. Do you want us to prepare everyone's meals every morning? I asked again because I could not understand.

"What? You want us to prepare our own breakfast?"

"Yes, you red pigs will have to prepare all of our meals. This is for the time being."

"Chuck, are you saying this out of your mind? How can we prepare this large group of meals?"

"I think you can do it enough. Do not say anything else and follow my decision. Or you can leave this place."

"You're right. That will do. He is our boss! Do you have any other ideas?"

I could hear sounds everywhere from the sly Panky's words. Of course, most of the sounds were just sympathetic to Chuck's words.

"We'll agree with Chuck, too. The price should be paid to those who disturb the order here. Otherwise, we cannot stay together. Of course."

The youngest group of pigs, who were brown strangers like Mr. Dali, suddenly spoke. He began to hurl vicious words at us without hesitation.

"Look at the cunning of the red pigs. They made me do all kinds of errands, treating me like a child. He even told me to go out and see if there was any leaking point on the wall on a rainy day. I was angry at the time, and they completely ignored me because I was a child. Those selfish, greedy pigs have no reason to live with us. If they don't follow Chuck's rules, we'll have to kick them out of here."

Mr. Dali grabbed him by the shoulder and stepped up to

restrain his word.

"Tim! I do not think it is your business. This is the work of adults. You are still too young to understand each other. I mean, you could be hated by those red pigs."

"Mr. Dali, I just said it because I have something to say. Otherwise, I was confused and I just could not stand it. Nevertheless, it does not change my mind. Without those crowds, this place would be really peaceful."

Now that even the young man had come forward and ignored our red pig masses, I could not stand the disgusting atmosphere. Since when have we been treated like this here? I asked myself a question. However, I could not find the answer anywhere. It was not our decision that our group chose this place. It was also questionable whether there was a place to go when we left here. Nevertheless, we cannot just leave here as if we are being kicked out. This is a matter of our pride. I looked at the red pigs around me.

They all looked foolish. There was no one in sight to challenge this difficult situation. They seemed to have learned from Chuck's authority. No, it was like a domestic slave who could not find our identity here. I was hoping that anyone would take sides on behalf of the red pigs in this situation, but I do not think so. Jack and I looked into each other's faces and only stood blank for a moment how to interpret the situation.

He looked at me to say anything, but not a word came out of my mouth. Just thoughts in my head were listed dizzily as words. They were such things as confusion, embarrassment, nausea, or burning anger like a volcano. I saw the faces of the red pigs around me. All of them became dumb in this situation with their bloodshot eyes. My poor comrades! Is this the last place we' or do we have to show that we are breathing together? Things were not that bad until a little while ago. At least not until Chuck appeared.

It has always been a problem with this Chuck. We have to overcome this heavy pressure. All the species in the world would have been free before being dragged by someone. They have been taught. To be domesticated, like to use an ass. I opened my mouth carefully. Just I began to speak towards the wide and wrinkled face of the white Chuck.

"Chuck, how do we interpret this situation?"

"You don't understand me yet. I am punishing you red pigs. The punishment's right, it is a price that you have broken down my order here."

"What order have we broken? We were just so hungry that we asked Sally if there was any food that left us. Is that guilty?"

"I am not going to blame you. Nevertheless, I have heard all your conversations outside, though Panky has explained the situation. Your attitude was not polite. You gave us orders as if you were kings here. Even though this boss is still here. That's your fault."

"Chuck, we didn't order. We just asked. We all know that they do not usually look at us in a good point of view and try to kick us out without missing this opportunity. You cannot do this. It's rather like you're breaking the peace here."

"What? Are you arguing with me? If I do it, you guys can just obey. This is the law here. I'm Chuck's law."

"I think we need to negotiate. I cannot follow your offer or order right now. I don't think it's up to me to decide it alone because we have to discuss it."

"Then I'll give you time for discussing until tomorrow. You guys can decide tomorrow and start the day after tomorrow. I'll wait until tomorrow."

You will give me time to think by tomorrow. You are giving a completely one-sided order. This group does not need any more round tables. Compromise and mediation are gone.

I felt compelled to accept their proposal. I had to gather the red pigs tomorrow and decide what we should do in the future.

"All right, Chuck, we'll discuss it among ourselves and give you an answer by tomorrow evening."

"What decision? You just have to obey." He suddenly muttered cynically and went out with his followers.

I looked at the back of Chuck. He looked as if he wanted us to just leave. He thought as if we are a nuisance. He might have guessed that we would not accept his request. That may be why we have made unreasonable demands that we simply cannot keep up with. Despite his old age, his ideas were like very crafty old foxes. He knew the red pigs would not comply with his terms. I also did not know how to interpret this ridiculous situation. Turning from his back, I said to the rest of groups.

"I have a favor to ask, but only a bunch of red pigs remain here and get the rest out of here. I have something to discuss with you."

Brown strangers and black pigs went out one by one. Only

the red pigs were left. There was a large, long table, so I suggested they sit down and discuss it.

"Let's sit here and discuss it with each other. This is a very important matter, with the fate of our red pigs at stake."

"Jim, this is a problem that we can't let go of. Our pride is at stake. How can a boss us be framed and kick out without thinking about protecting his flock? I really don't understand."

Jack was angry and said aloud at the table. The number of red pigs gathered at the table seemed to be about 15. The ratio was about 10 percent compared to the total number. There was the oldest red pig in the group. His name was Luzon. He was the oldest to settle down here. He slowly began to speak, fiddling with his long beard on both sides.

"I think our Red Pigs are out of their sight. We stand before two choices. Is one going to stay? Alternatively, are we going to leave? I've decided to stay here."
All of a sudden, his words made everyone's eyes flutter.

"What's the point of saying that all of a sudden, Luzon?"

"It doesn't do us any good to go out here right now. I have been living here for a while, and where would I go if I left now? In addition, being kicked out of the place like this is no example for our young descendants. I think we need to find our rights back here."

"That's right! Luzon is right. I cannot go on like this. Let's find our lost rights again!" Most of what Luzon said was in favor.

"Then what should we do? To find our rights."

"In addition to looking for rights, we're masters of this

place."

"What?"

Everyone's eyes were dazzled with astonished. It was a revolutionary remark. You think we are masters of this place. It was unthinkable. Luzon unhesitatingly uttered the word in front of us. Jack and Jim hit the ball as if they were in full agreement with him.

"Luzon! Your words are my words. You got the point right."

"Jim, I knew what you were thinking earlier. You and Jack have always been unhappy about this place. I just pretended not to know. I think it is time for us to act now. We cannot live on their errands forever. The question is how to plan and act. If our Red Pigs join forces together, we will be able to position ourselves here."

"Okay, Luzon, I talked to Jack last time. I think Chuck is too old to judge, and he is not very healthy. We wanted to make the rumors about him bad and spread them."

"Creating a bad rumor about Chuck? What kind of rumors are you talking about it?"

"Given his dim memory and weak health, I don't think he'll live long. This is the time to take advantage of his weakness. Fortunately, the poor white pigs are still under the delusion that he will stay in power for a long time. I think if we are going to trap him, we are going to have a false rumor that he has been stealing food from the warehouse secretly, eating himself full, and giving us food like trash. Those who are sensitive to food will feel bad about Chuck if they think he has been secretly taking good food and they have eaten junk food. That is the chance. If we keep creating worse rumors, they will end splitting up. That's when our Red Pigs rebel and drive them out of here at once."

Luzon suddenly rose from his seat and said excitedly.

"That's a very good idea. Jim, I think there is a good chance for us, too, if you think so. So when do we do this?"

"First of all, we have to slow their guard, preparing breakfast for them from tomorrow morning, as they demand. We can do it slowly for a few days and do what we wanted."

"Okay, let's do it."

It has already been a deep night since I finished talking. We decided to go back to our separate quarters for the next day. I looked up at the night sky. Countless galaxies were about to pour down the ground. The night breeze blew and it made me feel as if it would make me forget the heat of the day for a moment.

Look those who have the boundary between holiness and deceit, and those who are too pure to measure their distance. A premature infant who does not know who their mother is takes a breath in the corner of the street. For those who are on border, and who will follow them into an endless abyss, always have no idea which side to stand on.

Someday this place will be a place that may disappear as well. Where no one can remember, like hell, full of quarrels, timing, competition and greed. However, that is something that is going to take a very long time. Fortunately, memory will not last as long. It may be the best option to overcome the pain as often as you forget it.

We cannot fool each other in the unconscious world where memory grows. If that happens, they will soon be on their own path of ruin.

Their memories will be terrible screams and promises there.

Memory gives way to arrogance and is brainwashed. Whatever happens, it always acts as a perfect actor in any situation, with a weapon trained in its terrifying excuses and extreme arrogance for itself. All that survives will be nothing more than a vain, sometimes sad and convivial play on stage. Sometimes I see the back of those who leave here early in the morning.

Where they were headed in a moment when no one was awake, their shadows were always heavily laid on the ground, and the long dark rugs stretched to where we were staying.

It was a horror scene. No one asked why about it. Their memories might have been brainwashed or because they did not want to know everything.

Their long queue of rotten, drooping potatoes and the old food scraps someone ate was like a chorus for the dead gathered at the funeral. It was a parade of incompetent leaders and brainwashed idiots who lost their boundaries that they might not know where to stand. This scorching heat never seemed to end easily. One summer night's heavy rain and thunder made the nerves sharp as the intensity was added. The smell of blood seeping through the prickly gums also shook the instinct of the sleeping beasts to wake it up.

In their primitive and unbroken altar, trials take place every day to bring down the death penalty. As death has become a daily routine, its beautiful senses have died and only tainted ideas, such as the stench of the sewers, have dominated.

The skin-white pigs here learn from the same species with

exceptional ability by asking and answering themselves and assuring themselves every day, questioning themselves that they are the best bloodline. They always bragged that they were the best species in the world. They talked that we are not a descendant of the barbarians and the most superior and not below others, always reigns over others, and is a power-wielding clan.

No one was willing to refute the glistening words like heavenly stars. It was because they were also tamed by their bravado. I had to put up with the terrible smell of sweat in the middle of summer.

No one knows what made them so. While we were here, the atmosphere overwhelmed us all. We cannot be called slaves, but we have not yet to feel free.

Their sanctuary was always changed. It was always our turn to eat after they ate first. The hardest place for cleaning was our duty, and even we had to repair the leaking ceiling. We all did not complain.

Inequality has also become an obligation. The place where they lived was the best place here. Especially, it did not leak even when it rained, and it was a warm place, not cramped when many lay down. It was a great place compared to where we lived. They proudly said that it was because they deserved it. We could not make any excuses. No one knew what they were talking about at night. We just had to move as directed. That was the rule.

No one could fight back or oppose an unjust order. Autocracies are irresponsible rulers to make unconscious fools or irresistible children. Until now, we had only dreamed of living in a tomb-like place with little hope.

Where there is always something to eat, there must be troublesome beings like flies. There's always something attached around them like flies, where they wield absolute power like stupid Panky. Moreover, another example is a group of red monkeys that came in from an island.

They are a group that always sticks to the strong, makes all kinds of flattery, and lies. There are very different species of pigs mixed together. It was all part of the effort to drive us out when there was some sort of agreement between them.

They were controlled by force, entrust the soulless body to the flow of power. Maybe they are the most dangerous beings. There are such cowardly beings in any group.

Black pigs, white pigs, red pigs, brown strangers, they have these too. It is a place where we have to adapt to the environment as if it were a strategy to survive. A careless mind is a guide to extinction and enslavement. It was they, not us, who broke the silence.

No offerings were prepared for the festival. Those who take up the champagne first anyway will open any space that cannot be shared. This is not a game, it is survival.

It is a fight to preserve the species. A strategy meeting was needed, but what is needed before then is justification. The reason for doing this had to be clear. This cause will be an important tool to persuade other red pigs.

The cause is clear, because you have to survive without being kicked out of here. No one wants himself or his family to be threatened with survival for no reason. That is our cause.

That night we did not have to persuade each other. We got unanimous consent. Never before have we been so united in hearted this made no problem in developing and proceeding with the next plan. Rather, it was a question of what to choose because of the pouring of ideas. Perhaps they will make their own plans to drive us out. Maybe join forces with other groups.

Before the storm, silence prevailed here, just as the atmosphere was always quiet. Each of them was holding their own meeting.

Crossing the broad courtyard, there is a large space where white pigs are clustered next to a pile of hay. It was well built with red bricks, and the ceiling was so solid that it would not leak. The door to the place was always locked. There was always a small hole in front of the door to check in. When someone knocked on the door, they wanted to see who was outside. Lights were leaking through the windows there. Although the curtains were obscured, the incandescent light that leaked through them remained unabated and shone outside. In addition, sometimes there was a shadow on the window. The size must have been Chuck. The sight of his legs hurt came into our sight in shadow. He seemed to make a speech, gathering his men in a slightly excited tone.

"You shouldn't pretend to be noble in front of our interests. This is a matter of connection to our survival. Look at the dignity of our white pigs. You should always be proud of our descendants, how proud they are how else could they live here enjoying the privilege? You should know that all of this is because of me. I, this Chuck has been leading you with excellent leadership. I know I am not young enough. I will have to retire soon, but I do not want to back down like this way. Because we need a more solid status of our white pigs. Therefore, I am going to choose my successor among you. Because if we hand over leadership to other pigs, all our powers that we have accumulated so far are at stake. For me, the next boss should come out of the white pigs. However, there is a dissenting voice in front of this big plan! Do you know who they are?"

Not even a white pig, but a cunning imitator, Panky suddenly came to the side of Chuck and began to make a loud noise.

"It's the red pigs, to say the least, especially Jack that controls Jim from behind."

"You're a very smart guy, too, Panky. How you're not even like a pig, but you're destined to be in the same boat with us, aren't you?"

Panky clung closer to Chuck and whispered in his ear.

"Actually, I don't have anywhere else to go. No one is accepting me. Everyone thinks I'm a traitor..."

"Well, yeah, don't worry. Panky, I will keep you to the end, unless you are just betraying us. You must be a loyal dog by my side until I am old and pass this position on to someone. Do you understand?"

"Boss, I'm a dog. I have been a dog since I was born. It's a house-guarding dog."

"All right, Panky, if you always hear the information we need, you should let me know without delay. Okay?"

"I see. Do not worry. I will be your foot and ears. Of

course, it's the mouth."

He started drooling with his white teeth.

"Now come up with a brilliant idea. A way to get those Communist bastards out of here."

"They're not going to do the breakfast we've already suggested for us. You do not have to wait any longer then. We can get them out of here by the hands of gangsters right now."

"Gangster? Who should I hire?"

"We need to coax the black pigs here to join us in this."

"What do you do to kick them out?"

"They're not going to sit back and be beaten. They will have a meeting of their own. We cannot wait. We have to act first."

"That's a good idea. In addition, after they get out of here, we can put the order back in order. Then let's see how they come out tomorrow morning."

"Yes, boss."

"I'm against Panky's opinion!"

Suddenly, a young pig named Lille raised his hand. Among the white pig groups, he was a very young and strong man now in adulthood. Whenever he had a chance, he was trying to gain the upper class among the white pigs.

"Why does the boss always listen to Panky? Please listen to our opinion."

"Oh yes, Lille, I was just waiting for your opinion. Do not blame me. Tell me. Lille! What should we do?"

"They're very cunning group. They will not step back easily. It is bound to strike back. If we physically force them out, we could be attacked."

"Oh! Revenge and counterattack?"

"Yes, it is. Therefore, if we drive them out for no reason, public opinion will turn against us. We do not get support from other groups. We need to send them out for the right reasons. We have to give them time to leave."

"Lille, what do you think of the suggestion that we use the power of other pigs to drive them away? For example, with our white pigs, black pigs, and brown strangers."

"That's a good idea, but I'll have to unite with them. We need to ensure that they have a good profit."

"Well... profit?"

"They'll be interested in our proposal, too. They'll never want to lose anything."

"What kind of profit do you guarantee?"

"There may be a lot of things. Maybe we would like to make sure that after we eat delicious food first, our turn goes to them the next time. Alternatively, they can be assured that they are safe. Everyone knows that we white pigs have great power. Anyone would want to share some of that power with a group that is on our side. We can use them without having to struggle. We just need to sit back and watch. We don't have to put blood on our hands."

"I think it's a very good idea. Now I will have to call out leaders from other groups besides the red pigs. We need to have a meeting in secret once."

Lille looked at Panky and said,

"Panky, you go and bring the leaders here, one by one, among the black pigs and the brown strangers. Just tell them we have something to say. Okay!"

"I see, I'm going to go get it right now."

Autumn is not yet near, but the cries of small bugs were heard louder in the grass forests.

It was the cry of the crickets. There was a little commotion in the yard. In the lighted shed, someone was chattering. No one could sleep that night. There were only complaints and arrogant voices here and there, probably because of the high humidity and the noise of bugs and the acute tension of pigs.

The huge body and molars on the moon's shadow clearly resembled the shape of a monster. It was a grotesque and terrifying figure, with a lot of discontent and something unknown in it. The size and occasional bumping of stone pieces, which grew on the ground, was reminiscent of an army. The forthcoming storm, bloody battlefields, and howling cries, the most brutal tyrants and the most foolish of fools, came to mind. Running away was not the best option for them. The meanest, most benevolent, was a sort of ritual-like procession of things walking toward a bewitching death.

A wall of red bricks was visible. Old moss was growing through cracks in several places.

It was a barn built a long time ago. One side of the roof had a small hole, through which the moonlight was shining on the floor of the warehouse.

Just like a scene in a play, the curtain has risen and the audience is paying attention to the actors' performances. There were black pigs sitting around Chuck called Boss. In addition, right next to it were brown strangers, snobbish Panky, a bunch of monkeys who liked to join in everywhere.

No one brought up the story first. It is as if someone should start a conversation first. The black pig Sally opened her mouth first.

"Actually, I couldn't stand those red pigs for a long time. I do not know where those things came from. I think they are ignorant ones who do not know how polite they are. They always complain. I try my best to make food, but they always complain that it is not what they want because it is not delicious. They are very unlucky. They did not pay for anything. I am in favor of getting them out of here. On behalf of our black pigs, I will help you drive them out of here. How can I help you?"

Panky went on, agreeing to Sally's.

"Thank you, Sally, that's a lot easier for you to talk to. The boss and I talked to the white pigs to get rid of the prickly eyes at once. We have already agreed to kick them out without just looking. Nevertheless, our strength is not enough. We need your help. That's why I brought you here."

"All right. We will fully comply with your opinion. However, one thing I want to know is if we black pigs stand on your side, what are the benefits of us? We should have some benefit, shouldn't we?"

Chuck slowly opened his mouth with his hands together.

"Of course, we've thought through it the benefits that will give to you. I'll have to hear what you guys want."

"First of all, I want to hear what you white pigs think. You cannot just use us, and we cannot be kicked out like red pigs. We need to be prepared for every possibility. If we go along with your work, we need to hear the answer to what we're going to give us as a gift."

"Oh, come on why are you being so picky? Is that because you don't trust us?"

A group of monkeys from the island, who sat quietly in the corner, suddenly began to make noise. One of them, the chief, stuck to the side of Chuck and opened his mouth, shaking his red face.

"Don't worry, Sally. Chuck, our boss, does not steal the profits that he will give you from the middle. A bunch of us monkeys has already decided to join the white pigs' plan. You will have to decide which side to take, Self-destruction or co-existence? Hee-hee"

"Why are these monkey pups suddenly getting in the middle? Shut up quietly and go to the corner!"

"What, you bastards! Don't you see anything in sight of these black pigs? Why should we keep quiet?"

"This is a place where only pigs live? However, the monkeys, the puppies, are spending our food. In addition, you guys are so cunning. We cannot believe you. We all know how much you are betraying boss while we are away. You bastards! I'm talking to the boss right now and I don't want to talk to the red monkeys from the island."

"What? We will watch your doing how long you will be here."

The monkeys all got out of the room. As they went out, the rest heard a sudden loud shut of the door.

"Bang" Chuck began to soothe the black pigs.

"Look at this, Sally and our close associates! Why are you being so picky? We have been doing great. We discussed it together in times of need, and we became one. It is time for us to join forces again. There is nothing to benefit from the fight between us right now. If anything, the red pigs will like it."

"That's a story we all know. Why do you keep trying to get out of the point? We are just paying you to join your plan. What can we get?"

Suddenly Chuck was silent. He turned to the wall for a moment and seemed to be thinking of something.

For a long time he stood there, and for a moment, there was a heavy silence in a room. No one brought up the story first. Chuck again turned his head to the crowd, opened his mouth, and began speaking.

"Nobody has trusted and followed what I say so far, and now my heart is very distressed and sad. You do not trust anyone. I am a white pig boss, which always keeps my word. Nevertheless, if you black pigs want to hear a clear answer, well, if you cooperate with our work, you will be ranked second here right now. After our white pigs, you will gain status and power. But if you don't cooperate, you'll be kicked out of here like the red pigs."

His words caused some agitation among the black pigs. Moreover, Sally began to speak again.

"Boss, can you take responsibility for what you say? If we work together, can you really give our black pigs that power? If you can, we'll join your plan right now."

"Of course! I'll take responsibility for that as a boss."

As soon as he was finished speaking, the brown strangers on the right suddenly became angry and began to protest.

Suddenly the atmosphere of the room was turning more noisy and acrimonious. The brown strangers all tried to leave with discontent. Dali broke his silence and spoke. Then the young Tim began to sympathize with him.

"You're right, Mr. Dali. The reason we are here is that we are working together to make plans to drive out the red pigs. However, why do they treat us like ghosts? They don't listen to us at all, they just want to listen to the black pigs over there, and they are going to benefit them a lot? This is a very unfair and dirty treatment. There is no reason for us to be here. Let's all go!"

Suddenly the atmosphere of the room was turning more noisy and acrimonious. The brown strangers all tried to leave with discontent.

"Stay there. Where are you going? It's not over yet." Chuck called them up to go out of the room in an angry voice.

"If you leave without any ending like this, I won't deny that you will enemies against us. If you go out, our relationship with you will end here. We are not going to be responsible for any of the dangers that come to you. Do what you guys want?" As soon as Chuck had finished speaking, suddenly they turned their heads and looked at him in unison. Their eyes were not that elated look we had seen before. They looked puzzled. Chuck tried to affirm his words once again.

"I'm telling you again, if you guys get out of here, it's over with us. In addition, we are going to think of you as some of those bad red pigs. Moreover, you will all be kicked out of here. If you don't mind, get out of here right now!"

There were no pigs to contradict him. They were looking at each other's faces and just looking at each other. After a while, the youngest Tim of them gathered them in a small voice.

"Wait minute, brown strangers here! Come over here. I need to talk to you." From big hips to skinny ones, the brown pigs came around Tim.

"We're not going to end here, we need time. I'd like to say that we'll have this meeting adjourned for a moment." Chuck looks at them and smiles at them.

"Yeah, great! I cannot give you time for a long time. Hurry up and decide. I'll give you 10 minutes from now."

"I see."

Tim called their colleagues together, and for a moment, they began to enter the small room like garret, which had broken door in corner. It was a room close enough to hear everything outside because there was no door. All were cramped to get in, so some pigs even had their hips out.

They sat around both sides with young Tim in the middle. He began to tell firstly as if he were a leader.

"I don't think we're in a good situation. We are in no good if we leave like this. I do not think it will be too late to argue with us after we have agreed with them and driven out all the red ones. I don't think we need to hurry."

"Tim, the black pigs have already gotten enough for the meeting. However, there is nothing to say about us. It is like telling us to sacrifice unilaterally. I can't join them in their plans."

For a time it was John who was reticent among the brown pigs.

"John! Do not worry. I have an idea and a plan. We're not going to sit back and get hurt."

"Tim! Is that true? Can I take your word for it?"

"Yes, believe me; it will never hurt our group."

"If we cooperate, let's take this opportunity to split up the territory here and give us the area we can live in. The area where no one else can get in there but us and only our flock can survive. I think there is a place across the warehouse where they can store large grains, and let us ask for it. It is big enough and nice enough for our brown herd to live in. Give us there, and we'll cooperate with them."

"Well, that's good, but I need to talk to Chuck first. I'll give them a suggestion first."

"All right, and then let's do that."

The meeting was carefully dismantled and then brought back to Chuck's place. The night was not so deep yet. The crescent moon was faintly hanging in the middle of the mountain across. Sometimes there was a cool night breeze. It seemed to have let me forget the heat of the day for a moment. No one seemed to be in the mood to talk first. They just winked at each other first in the hope of bringing up the story first. For a moment, the air in the room began to cool down. The night wind began to blow through the cracks in the collapsed wall. The first thing to start talking was Dali

"Chuck, we talked for a moment about our future, and this is the conclusion. Before I bring up the subject, I'd like to ask if you're really friends with us to the end."

"Dali! I do not understand what you are talking about. Can you make it easier for me to talk to you again?"

"I mean, we can't trust you white pigs. That means that if we help you with your plan, we can be kicked out like the red pigs. So we want to know if you can protect us for certain."

"Dear Dali, there's nothing to worry about if it's a problem. I'll assure you, what do you want, just come up with your suggestions."

"Okay, Chuck, we discussed it among ourselves, and we came to a conclusion."

Chuck suddenly hit the table and talked loudly.

"Look, don't say conclusion. The bottom line is not yours, but I, the boss. Do not make me angry; otherwise, I am too old to stand up straightly. You know when I get angry, my blood pressure goes up." "I see. I will tell you from now on. It is our proposal. When the plan is completed successfully, please allow us to live among ourselves in the areas we want. We just want to live in a safe place."

"What?"

Chuck thought for a moment, perhaps the place to give to the orchard and us will have to bear a huge loss for them. Surely, this was something they should not give up. It was because if all of their demands were met, all of the harvests coming out of this place would be significantly affected and the influence of the white pigs would be gradually weakened. Nevertheless, if they did not comply with their demands, they knew they could not do it by themselves to get rid of the red pigs.

"Well, we're just saying that we need a place to live among

48

ourselves here, a space where no one is interfered."

Chuck tried to keep his calm. However, his trembling voice could still feel embarrassed.

"You want your own place in this place. No one is interfering? So where are you guys thinking about? Say it."

"There's a large warehouse next to the orchard over there. We want to live there by ourselves, and please do not let anyone meddle in our affairs. We're also going to solve our own problems."

"So you want to eat most of the delicious apples from the orchard?"

"I'm not saying we're going to eat it all. We can share some. We need to take everything except what you consume."

Chuck thought for a moment, perhaps the place to give to the orchard and us will have to bear a huge loss for them. However, if they did not comply with their demands, they knew they could not do it by themselves to get rid of the red pigs. He seemed to be lost in thought, dragging his uncomfortable legs to the floor. Then Panky seemed to approach him cautiously and whisper something.

"Boss! What are you thinking about so much? Just do as they ask. We need to put out the urgent fire right now. We cannot do anything on our own. First, we have to use a win-win strategy to make each other good. We are united now, but we can break our promise once we have done it successfully. Take their hands. We'll take care of the rest."

"How do you mean we're going to fix it? It's too much for us to come out like that already."

"Don't worry. By then, you can borrow the other guys'

hands and kick those brown ones out of here. But now is the time to help each other."

"Well, I get it."

Chuck returned to his place, and called them up in the middle. There was a lot of tension. Slowly he put his sick legs on the chair and said,

"It is arthritis; it's getting worse now that I am older. Look, is there any wine left here that I drank? Nothing is better than wine to soothe the pain."

For a moment, Panky went into the kitchen and brought out wine in a cracked bowl.

"Boss, there's a little left here. Try it. The pain will be much better."

"Yes, thank you. I am the only one with Panky. Even though he is not a pig like us, he is sometimes more useful than the other dumb white pig. Ha-ha, yeah, repeat, our brown guests, what you said to us earlier." Their elated attitude a short time ago has completely changed. It was like the images of a young child urinating on the bed at night and being caught by his mother early in the morning. Chuck was very overwhelming the atmosphere in the room. He began to drool from his open mouth, tapping the table again with his big front paws. Long saliva, which seemed to fall to the floor at any moment, was seen as if it were swinging on his mouth. The figure was even terrifying.

"Look, I'm so tired right now. It is time to go to bed. I will listen to what you want. Talk to me again. I do not have enough memory. It's a habit of forgetting things quickly if someone doesn't check them."

"Boss, it doesn't require much, just give us a place to stay safe and free after everything's done. It is our own space without anyone's interference. Then we will actively participate in whatever you plan and do. This is exactly what we're asking for."

"Ah! That is the problem, the things you think desperately want. Thanks for reminding me. You do not have to worry about that. We will ensure your safety and your freedom of residence. Do not worry when the work is done well. I'll give you all the convenience, so there's only one condition."

"What is it?"

"Well, it's not a difficult request. You have to do everything we command. Only by when all the red pigs are chased out of here. Until then, you must obey our orders absolutely. Even if the lowest rank among our white pigs commands you, you must follow that way. In addition, one more thing, even though he is not a pig, you must obey my loyal henchman Panky's words. I will clean it up again. You brown strangers pigs come right under our white pig. That period is only until everything is worked out and the Red Communist Party is completely driven out of here. If you do, we will meet all your needs. What do you think? My suggestion."

As soon as I heard him, a small disturbance began to occur among the brown herd. Small voices began to be heard here and there.

'Look, do you think this offer makes sense?'

'No, something unimaginable happened. How do you mean we should obey to those white pigs? Even if it's all over by that time, it means we're supposed to be their slaves, and this is a very embarrassing thing.'

They did not seem to be able to get their opinions together. As such, the offer by Chuck was somewhat shocking. A moment passed. While we were talking for a moment, we could hear the sound of rain falling from the tin roof as if a shower had passed.

Dali of them seemed to put together all the opinions. He stood before Chuck on behalf of the herd and said,

"All right, Chuck, I'll take your offer. We will obey you and your herd just until the red pigs is out of here. And then I want you to listen to what we asked for."

"Of course, Dali and dear brown friends! From now on, we are all comrades in the same boat. We are colleagues with a mission to clean up the mess. Hahaha! Oh my gosh, let us have a big party together because of ended this meeting. Look at this. Everybody gets together over here?"

"Bring me something to drink. Do you have anything for drinking? I think I'll forget the summer heat if I drink this night!"

Panky and a few others went to the kitchen. The kitchen was messed up with leftover food waste, and inside the large, long oak tree barrel, there were left of rotting debris for a few days. It happened to see cracked water bottles in Panky's eyes. He went there and sniffed at the bottles.

"Wow, I think it's someone's leftover wine. I do not know who it is, but thank you so much; let us get it to the boss. We're having a party with this."

Panky carefully brought out the leftover wine so that it would not fall down.

"Boss, here the wine left. I think it'd be nice to have a party with this."

"Bring it this way. Let's taste it."

Chuck took the bottle and started drinking it.

"Well, that's a good drink; everybody gets together, and let's get our loyal servant from tonight, the brown pigs, together and have a drink."

In fact, wine was a luxury drink for pigs. For the poor, alcohol from barley was enough. The red wine made their faces red, and they seemed to resemble the red pigs. Perhaps it was too conceited of themselves, and already the moon seemed to be sitting on top of the dark mountains, laughing at the party of the drunk pigs. I ran to the window and closed the door.

Here and there, I could hear the giggles. Monkeys were also holding onto their bellies, waving their red hips and laughing. They were celebrating a victory as if they were kings here.

The old tin can was turned upside down and tapped with a wooden stick to make rhythm. Moreover, everyone danced to the rhythm and enjoyed the drunkenness.

What survives cannot be silenced; good and evil coexist in the lips that are always alive. Long torn mouth and sharp fangs were seen. It was the last song of those who did not even recognize the danger beyond their boundaries.

Everything you have enjoyed while staying inside the boundary falls into an abyss when you give it up. Strangers who came from far away became their utopia here.

Regions that cannot be kept, the miserable memories of all

that have gone by, there is no place to go, and this place imagines itself as their paradise and seeks to win. The heat of the midsummer night further ignited their excitement. Everyone began to dance naked.

He seemed to see the sexual immorality on the ugly altar and of the wicked false priests. In the distance, I could hear a familiar bell. Maybe there is a ritual going on for someone somewhere.

A ceremony for the abandoned, soon they will have a new dawn. This is where it should be abandoned, but as long as they are here, this ugly ritual will be repeated every day.

I will have to wear a different mask when it dawns again. If I follow a mask that is parasitic on my face, it will have to follow a brain cell and have a day of delusion that seems to have become one cell. It was not just the days that were so perfect. It just seemed like the tension was making it that way. They seemed to have succeeded by constantly hypnotizing themselves that they were not pigs.

It was reminiscent of the rebellions of angry creatures living in different territories, of the servants who killed their master and took possession of the farm.

They were disgusting creatures, like the images of pirates floating on the sea trying to dominate everything. How will they act the next day after the mysterious night? As all the storms had foreseen, suddenly the wind from the middle of the mountain stopped to make such a foretaste. Even the leaves could not be seen shaking.

Like a dead time, they all fell into the silence, all drunk and snoring everywhere. The pigs here are not just idling around doing nothing. They have their own set order and have work to do when the day comes. For example, white pigs usually go from place to place, giving instructions. No one has so far defied what they said. The fact that they occupied this place first naturally put them in the top tier. Above all, Chuck was at the center of it. Because Chuck was a white pig, they acted as if they were nobles here.

Black pigs worked mostly in the kitchen, while other pigs picked up food from the mountains or stole it from other places across the border.

As in any group, there were monkeys from the Far East Island, and Panky abandoned by their owners, who took their own interests while making flattery by grasping the situation in moderation among them. It was an order created by them. They were slaves of order that no one could resist.

The order will repeat when tomorrow comes. However, tonight, there was already a conspiracy to break this order, and no one could say for sure what was going to happen.

Ch 4

After their own night, they spent a few nights more.

I felt as if those days had passed months. Life here has not always felt the same as any other day.

I had never experienced countless things in a day. Repeated routine dulls the senses, but when so many things happen in different places at different times, the period feels very long.

During that time, the pigs moved busily from place to place. Perhaps something was going on between them.

When I woke up, there was silence around me. I could not hear the sparrows in the trees. Where did they all go?

When I opened the door and went out, I could not see the hens in the yard. It was a strangely quiet morning. Sitting at the rotten root of a tree for a while looked at the distant mountain.

Sometimes I could feel the smell of manure fermented for compost at the tip of my nose, but it was bearable. A couple of hours later, loud voices began to be heard from beyond the wall. It was the voice of the red pigs, for they were seen through the holes of the fallen wall.

"Jack, how long do we have to do this? It has already been a week. This morning I went near the neighboring village reservoir and picked these rotten potatoes. Other red pigs also have a lot of complaints."

"Jim, let's hang in there a little bit. We have to wait a few days to get our work done yet. But it takes time for the rumors we spread about Chuck to get into everyone's ears."

"It's already been three days since I spread the rumor. However, there is no reaction yet. What the hell is going on Maybe the white pigs had heard the rumor first and blocked it from spreading further in the middle?"

"Maybe not. If they did, Chuck would already call us in and threaten us or kick us out. From the still quiet, I don't think they know."

"If the white pigs find out first, the plan will be ruined. Rumors should spread to black pigs or brown strangers. That way, we can revolt together and drive out the white pigs at once."

"You're right Jim; we can't deal with dictators on our own as yet. Let us wait one more day.

Maybe something will happen here tomorrow. If our opinions are well communicated to them, they'll come to us first to discuss countermeasures."

"All right, let's wait just one more day. I think there are grapes picking event this afternoon, so let's take a look at their reaction then."

It seemed like the time had come to pick grapes. The timing of the harvest seemed to be faster this year than the previous. It did not seem to have rained so much this year, considering the reason.

The hot weather continued every day. There were many days when there was a lot of sunshine. For grapes to be tasted deliciously there must be adequate sunlight. There were many such days this year. Thanks to good weather, it was hot summer. Our pigs enjoyed a leisurely nap while sitting in the shade of the vine eating grape fruit.

Nevertheless, there were very few such days this year. Conflict was the reason among the pigs.

I forgot to eat grape fruit to fight each other. Nevertheless, I am not going to let it go today. I thought I should eat enough grapes that I had never eaten before. Not only me, but also all the pigs here are probably thinking the same thing. Time seemed to run too fast for a few days as if to laugh at a short life. The more often grape trees harvest, the more thick the tree trunk becomes.

However, all the cunning animals here become simpler and lighter like feathers as time goes by. Just as instinct alone tries to survive, understanding and consideration become scarce. All get angry at nothing around me.

Once I inadvertently stepped on the feet of a white pig. Then suddenly, he attacked with a sudden angry look on his face. I explained that it was a mistake, but it did not work. It did not work to say sorry. I was beaten on the spot. The reason is that I stimulated himself to want stay still. I have never met anything like this before.

I thought about the reason why such a sensitive little thing easily stimulated them. It was also because of conflicts with red pigs and other beasts.

Since then, it has become unwritten law here not to trust anyone. Everyone had a feeling of becoming evil to survive. A loud noise was heard outside the door. The owner of the voice could not know who it was, but the loudest voice was to bring the pigs into the yard.

"Look at this! We are all gathering in the yard. What if you take a nap after lunch? You have a lot of work to do this afternoon. Do not sleep in peace. Let us go pick some delicious grapes. Everybody's got to the outside!"

"I know, I was going to take a long nap."

All of them were filled with complaints. There is always a fixed amount of time to take a nap after lunch.

However, we have to go out to the vineyard today. Everyone seemed to hate to go, but when they thought they could still eat delicious grapes, they came out and began to gather in the yard. The number in the yard seemed to be about a hundred. However, no one could see the red pigs.

Chuck's messenger Panky climbed onto the rock in the yard. Then he looked down for a moment and said,

"Come on, get together this way. So I can see your face from here."

Everyone gathered around the rock without responding to his words. They followed his order and began to move like a brainwashed robot without any resistance.

"Let's see, who's not here. My eyes can't fool anyone."

Panky looked around with his eyes wide open. Then suddenly, in an angry voice, he shouted.

"No, no, no, no! I cannot see any red pigs. Where did they all go? Somebody tells me if you know about this!"

There is a moment of silence. In addition, some pigs said aloud.

"The red pigs are not coming to pick the grape fruit this afternoon. They told me. From now on, they won't follow the orders of the white pig."

"What?"

Panky asked, with a look of disbelief.

"Who can explain this situation to me so that I can understand it easily?"

"They're not coming back here again. I heard it."

"What's the reason?"

"You know better. Maybe they won't be with us, and they'll be independent of themselves."

"Independence?"

"Yes, and asked no one to interfere."

"Then they have to get out of here right now? How can we live together in one place?"

"They said no to it. They just don't want to face us."

Panky seemed to go for a moment and discuss the matter with Chuck. Then he climbed up the rock again and began to speak.

"All right, I'm going to deliver Chuck's message from now on. Listen to me, everybody the red pigs are no longer our companions. After this day, we are going to expel them from here. In addition, when you run into them, you will never say hello and ignore them. They cannot even sit at the table and eat with us. We will give them a week, so if they do not get out of here right now, we will throw them out with force. So far, it has been Chuck's order."

I heard a murmur among pigs. The situation seemed to change seriously. When the red pigs find out about this, they will make a big fuss. In this situation, the only way to survive is to stay on the strong side. I heard a small whisper. There was simply no reply to that remark. I heard the sound of Panky again.

"Now let's all go to the vineyard. We have a lot of work to do this afternoon."

Panky began to divide the work as if he were a captain.

"You bring a basket, and you pick grapes here. Do not be lazy and harvest your own amount until sunset. Got it?"

His words were too one-sided. It is as if we do not follow the order, or we will suffer a great loss. Everyone started to be busy like a robot picking grapes. The vineyard was not far from the yard. Just past one wall, a large vineyard began.

The fruit that was not yet harvested was ripe and fell to the ground. Some pigs were busy sitting and picking up fruit that had fallen to the ground, not thinking about putting grapes in a basket. Their faces became red with the taste of ripe grapes, and they felt like they were getting drunk.

It seemed like a couple of hours had passed. Everyone began to slip out of the vineyard. With a fat body, they began to gather in the yard with a basket full of grapes. In the middle of the yard was a large wooden box that could hold dozens.

"Put the grapes you've all brought into this barrel!"
When Panky spoke, everyone began to put the grapes in the can.

"We're going to make wine from now on. We all need to get in this barrel and step on the grapes. And we're going to put it back in the bin and take it to the warehouse."

As soon as the word spoke, the pigs went into the barrel and began to tread until the grapes were juicy.

It was a big event at the time of harvesting grapes. It was to make wine, store it, and drink it.

"Wow, this is the first time for so many grapes. Too many. We must be drinking enough wine this year. It is a great day. Unless it's just a red pig, we will be happy here!"

As soon as the word was finished, there was a loud noise from the back of the barn. It was Jack's loud voice. Perhaps it was the sound of the red pigs walking here. Jack began to speak loudly.

"You've collected a lot of grapes. Look, we did not go because we did not want to pick grapes. It is just that we did not participate in the grape-gathering event because we had work to ourselves. Do you understand?"

"Of course I understand. But you should also know that you can't enjoy wine together unless you pick grapes!"

At Panky's words, Jim and Jack and the red pigs gathered there were angry but could not answer back. Those who do not work do not eat. That was the right thing to say. They were red pigs who could not be seen until the grape harvest was over and the wine was done. In the eyes of other pigs, it must have been hateful. Jim, Jack, and other red pigs began to leave quietly, showing large molars. When they all disappeared from the yard, the night came. All the pigs gathered in a large warehouse and took out the wine they had made last year and began to celebrate. Of course, the red pigs were not able to participate there either.

Their presence was like dew to disappear in a moment that was soon forgotten.

"I'll see when your world continues here! You selfish

bastards! And you poor colored pigs who'll be fooled by them for life!" Jim stepped back and began to talk loudly.

"Maybe sooner or later, our world will come. It is too late then. We are not going to accept anyone. We will ignore no matter how hard you beg us. Now you and we are going to be completely enemies. You stupid idiots!"

The red pigs were swaying around like venomous snakes, perhaps hurt by their inferiority complex and self-esteem for not being able to eat wine. They were showing sharp and long teeth and a tendency to provoke a fight at any moment. After a few minutes, however, the surroundings were quiet, as if nothing had happened.

After they disappeared, the frantic party lasted until the early morning rooster crowing. So far, the red pigs have not slept at all. Perhaps now they have their own plans to end all this. A few red pigs were gathered in an empty area with many weeds.

"Jim, why is it so quiet? Did you ever spread a rumor about Chuck?"

"Of course, yesterday I told some of the white pigs that were talkative."

"What? No, when did you say you would make a rumor, and now you are telling them? Where and what have you been doing? Did you just play? With nothing to do?"

"I'm sorry, but I've been too busy."

"This is the fate of our red pigs. The plan to set a time after the rumor first spread out and attack and kill all of them overnight. Can you take responsibility for this? If they know first, and they attack us, we'll have to be killed!"

"Don't worry. Jack, in a day or two, every situation will be over. Half of them must have heard the rumor by now. Then we will have to get one by one of them to our side. Let's kill Chuck together then."

"By the way, what's the story of rumor? I am curious too. Can you tell me?"

"Not yet. You will know when you hear it in person. There's nothing good about gossiping out of us first."

It was not the red pigs who would just sit there and be beaten. It was evident that something was planned and going on between them. It has not been too long for everyone to know what is going on. They held big party with wine, and they were so drunk, lay down in the yard, and started to sleep. Such a life was repeated for a few days. As the day passed, some tension began to flow in their faces. It was as if some of them had spread and there was a growing mood of doubt about each other.

It was one morning after a few days. I could not hear the rooster crowing, which was usually announced early in the morning. It was such a quiet morning. I heard a murmur under a large zelkova tree in the back of the yard. There were white pigs, black pigs, and some other animals, brown strangers. Each was looking around, tense as if to notice the atmosphere. Everyone's face was not so bright. Something serious must have been happening. Panky was not also sitting for a while, repeatedly biting his fingernails as he circled around the chuck. His face was filled with discontent.

However, a hopeless situation did not seem to be resolved until no one spoke.

I heard a pig whispering, whose name was hard to remember.

"Did you hear the rumor?"

"Of course I heard it clearly. There are too many opinions among pigs now because of the rumor. I think they're trying to figure out the truth."

"I can't imagine this guy was the boss of this place, Chuck, a white pig. We have been tricked into living this whole time by him. I'm angry to think he cheated on us!"

"You know what? I didn't think so about Chuck either, but if the rumors are true, it's not the red pigs who should leave here right now, it's Chuck and his bastards."

"That's right, we can't just let that bastard live here. Everyone is out here right now because they cannot hold back their anger against Chuck. There's a reason he has to explain this rumor." Then there was a loud noise from somewhere.

"Chuck can't do this to us. He betrayed us!"

It was a sound from among the brown pigs.

"That's right, how can he betray us like this? There is no pig in the world to trust. How does he dare plan to exterminate all of us?"

"After all the red pigs have been removed, next it's our turn! Chuck and his servants had a plan to make the completely white pig world. We have just heard about this rumor. It's a good thing, isn't it?" "Now is the time for us to take concrete action. If that greedy Chuck, act doesn't explain anything."

"You're absolutely right. We are not the ones who will be left alone. Then why can't I see Chuck? I'm sure he's got a dirty plot to attack us."

It was then. A figure of Chuck emerged through the grass. His figure was haggard and looked very tired as if he had not slept last night. He had been struggling with his big body leaning on cane as if his legs that had been limping had become worse.

"What the hell are these sounds? Who's spreading lies I've never heard before? Come out in front of me right now. Let's see what his face looks like and see that cheeky face."

There were no pigs trying to answer Chuck's excited remarks. They just looked around, silently gazing around at his words. Chuck began to speak again.

"Did I say I'd kick out the red pigs or kill them and I'd get rid of the other pigs when this is over?"
For a moment, silence ruled the yard.

"No? Why aren't you saying anything? Anyone who can answer my question, show up here right now!"

It was then. The pig in front of Chuck was a black pig Sally. "Chuck, I don't want you to react like that. I do not think you are in this position right now. I do not think we can forgive your flock of white pigs for betraying us. If you really meant to bring us all down and get rid of us, we would not just sit back! I'd like to ask if all these rumors about you are true."

"Oh, my God, Sally! What are you talking about? Where did you hear that? You really think I'm going to do that?"

"Certainly, given what you've done so far, I think you and the white pigs will do enough. How have you behaved towards us so far? You have been treating us like a servant. It is as this is your country, and you are the king and we are your people. I don't think all these rumors are false."

Chuck's front feet were seen trembling. Perhaps he was stimulated by Sally's words. He began to rub his back against a large old tree for a while.

It seemed to be a gesture to shed the parasites on his back. When he got excited, it was an occasional show. Then he went on speaking.

"No matter how much I explain now, I think you've already been brainwashed by the rumor. Once again, all the rumors you have heard are false. I am innocent; let us get together here again in a few days. I don't think I can come to any conclusions right now." Sally began talking.

"You cowardly act, and now you're trying to run away. From now on, I'm going to negotiate with you on behalf of all the pigs left."

"Sally! How can you say that to me in person? Don't you think of our relationship in this place? I am the one who is allowed as many privileges as you have in this restaurant so far. In addition, you can stab me in the back of my head and betray me like this? I really don't understand your behavior."

"Chuck, don't get me wrong. It is just that we have to survive here, too! I will not listen to you from now on. From today, you must cook yourselves what you are going to eat at the restaurant. I am not even going to prepare a meal for you anymore. Except for our black pigs." Sally was the leader of the black pigs. Sally planned everything and they had only to obey her orders.

Sally's willingness to mix with black pigs was tantamount

to declaring independence from Chuck. Increasingly rumors were bringing a deadly trap. After that, everyone was going back to their own places and plotting their own lives. Perhaps a huge headwind would blow.

The red pigs were not there. For a long time that night, in a secret place that only they knew, the lamp had not been extinguished.

As if to celebrate what started with a half victory, everyone was talking in a jubilant way with their white teeth exposed.

"I've lived in this boring place so far, and today is the most rewarding and had a good day. Did you guys see that? Those stupid pigs were cheated and showed anger to Chuck. Jim, you could have told us earlier that this is your plan. You are a genius. I am proud that you are a red pig. Think about it. If your skin was white, we wouldn't be able to live here."

Jim, barely sitting in the chair with heavy and fat body, said after much thought.

"It's not over here. We have to push ahead a little more. We cannot afford to own this place by ourselves. I sent spies to the black pigs and the other herd. Maybe we'll hear from them in a little while."

"What's going on? Has it moved on already? Did they say they'd cooperate with our work?"

"Jack and our comrades! Let us wait a minute. There will be good news soon. After the spies I've sent here arrive, I'll talk about the specific plan and put it into practice."

The spies sent to them were faithful errands. The red pigs would have explained to them the privileges they would have enjoyed here one day, and they would gladly accept the offer and become the eyes, hands and feet of the red pigs.

In fact, red pigs were smarter and more cunning than white pigs, if they even bribed spies by playing the game first. They were always adept at adapting to the changes in the environment. Inside them, deep rebelliousness continued to spread like ivy, their performance was perfect, to the extent that they admired even the weakest on the outside and the false obedience.

I could see their eyes through the broken door. It was bloodshot eyes. They were a bunch of monkeys who stood beside the white pigs like wildcats.

Their source was a small island country in the east. The island was made of ancient volcanoes. No one knows how they got here, but what they did was a cowardly act of sticking to the strong and harassing the weak.

That was their way of survival. They knew they had nothing to expect from the white pigs, and now they are the hands and feet of the red pigs. The door opened and a group of monkeys suddenly pushed inside. Then they started talking in their own language, either on the table or on the shelf.

"Come on, quiet! Quiet!" The red pigs began to talk.

"Here, there are monkeys who have been allied with us for a while! Everyone looks at their faces once. They'll have something to tell us."

There was an unusually small group of monkeys with red cheeks. It has been a long time since I have forgotten his name, but he has always been an active, chatty and cunning guy.

"Now, all the rumors we've heard are from us. Now, of course, I think the owner of this place is the red pigs. Until now, our monkeys have always been the second ranked status pushed out by Panky and his gangs, but not anymore. We can have a power like them if we help the red pigs. That's why we volunteered to be your mouth and feet."

"Of course, I'll never forget your monkeys' doing. All right, if we get rid of all the white pigs, we will treat you monkeys here as the second ranked here. Rumor was a successful strategy to completely divide the white pigs and other groups. Now let us decide the date. It is a day when we can get rid of everyone at once and take over the place completely. If you have any suggestions, tell me now."

"First, let's call in the monkeys who went to the other pigs and listen to their opinions. Are you sure we're going to do together?"

"Of course, we told them what we wanted. They all agreed to join us. Do not worry about it. We can't beat the white pigs on our own, but if they're on our side, victory will be ours."

"For them, that would be an unbearable time of pain. To be clear, we are too weak compared to them. But if we borrow the strength of the pigs we already have, we can defeat them."

"Now, tell me your plan. What should we do and how?"

"Once in a while, they'll throw another big party to celebrate the harvest of grapes. We're going to put the powder that makes them drowsy into the wine."

"What kind of powder are you going to make?"

"Snowbell tree powder."

"Well, the tree has an anesthetic effect. That is when we are going to raid. It's a good idea."

The alliance between them was like a reckless gamble. Originally, pigs were a symbol of greed. Rumors about pigs were not so good, according to the old phrase.

It has been undeniable that it has been recognized as a symbol of cleaning staff, who usually dispose of food scraps from villages, or of the disgust of discharging dirty filth. It is funny that they dream of a revolution. However, as if their gaze had nothing to do with it, they seemed to celebrate the victory in advance, like the winner who had already won the battle. Now the story is running towards the end. One might end up with an easy-to-predict ending, but the story behind it might end up with shame.

Ch 5

*A*nyone can dream of a quiet revolution.

However, there is not that much chance of success. Nevertheless, there are indeed many reckless gamblers. Some idealists are making silent sacrifices and quietly disappearing to the back of their insignia. All those days of life vanish in vain, and once again, the curtain rises and ends on the stage, living on the sidelines like an audience that knows it will soon be over.

The revolution they dream of was not such a splendid or exciting thing. It was only a long procession of deaths that some planned so. This is what the Bible says.

One day comes the day when the owner of the farm has to make a long trip. However, he needed someone to take care of the farm while he was gone. They were servants. The owner asked his servants to take good care of the farm before he left. However, while the owner is away, the servants' mind begins to change. As if the owner of the farm were themselves, they pretended to be the owner of the farm and even stole his owner's things. They kill other people the owner sent to confirm and even kills the owner's son.

Eventually, after returning from the trip, the owner knows

all this happening and destroys them.

Who is the master and who is the slaves those who enjoy the game with unknown puzzles are seen in front of their eyes. It is time to finish this short story. Everything in the world runs toward the end. Have you ever waited for a train to rush in from platform on a harsh cold day?

You will have to find the boundary between the beast and the upright creatures. It is a simple dream for anyone to miss a cup of tea lying on a warm stove in the cold. You will have to refuse to be an animal from the depths of the inner world and calm your ever-rising desire for a civilized person.

Everything is hypnotized on its own in the delusion.

The day was so still and life continued as if nothing had happened to the mean place where they lived.

The pigs ate themselves, slept, and rolled around in the mud, enjoying the wine. When they came to their senses, they cut down the bamboo and began to make sharp spears or knives. The goods seemed to be intended for use on the day of revolution they called.

Their land has never been preserved for a long. The owner of the land changed during several hundred years. There was no permanent empire. Creatures will also disappear and occasionally be disassembled as fossils in a museum lab after thousands of years. They did not even know that. It was the night before the revolution. Still unable to interpret anyone's language, they were already preparing for the final blood festival there, grinding their teeth in the form of rebel forces.

On one side of the farm, we could see a two-story house built of oak, where the lamp's fire would not extinguish.

It was a white-haired man with a bent back that looked like it was old, with tangled hair. He looked too old to measure his appearance and age.

Next to him sat the old woman. Even inaudible, the man seemed to be speaking aloud in her ear, but the old woman was looking at the scene outside the window, which was darkened with no response at all to the sound. At that time, a middle-aged woman, who appeared to be his wife, brought a steaming chunk of meat to the table, as if she had just taken it out of the oven.

"Mom! Can you hear me? This is Uluru. Your son."

The old woman did not respond to his words. Obviously, she was suffering from dementia. She cannot remember his son's voice or face.

"Honey, that's enough! She cannot see and hear you. We cannot help it now that she is old. Do not waste your time. Come here and get some freshly baked pork. I caught a very young pig and baked it in the oven, and it's sweet and delicious."

There was steaming pig meat on the plate. Next to, it was a salt could. The man picked up the salt container and began to put it on the meat.

"My mother used to be as beautiful as a young woman, but now she's old and she's got Alzheimer's, I feel so sorry for her. However, what now? I can't decide everything on my own."

"What's wrong with you? Uluru?"

"It's all over the country right now with an ASF (African swine fever), pig fever."

"Piggy fever?"

"Right, that pig fever. There is a rumor that it has already crossed the Atlantic. This fever does not even have medicine. Once they get sick, they will be wiped out! Exterminate! Holy shit, I am going to have to quit this job right now. That is why I am going to ask my mom. However, my mother's opinion is important, so I cannot decide it alone because she has been doing it for a long time. What do you think?"

"Then we can sell them all before the fever arrives. In addition, let us leave this town together. Let us go somewhere else. We can find a new job there."

"Really, I'm sick of these pigs. And the smell is too bad, and I think it's time for us to go out and live in the city."

Uluru was listening to her silently. Still he seemed to mind the old woman. Nevertheless, we cannot delay our decision.

The swine fever has already come to the fore. We have to sell everything at a bargain price. In neighboring countries, all pigs are said to be dead and unseen. Pork was not found in the market at all, and even if it was lucky, it was too expensive for ordinary people to buy. It cost as much as $50 a kilogram.

"But what do we do with those monkeys when we get rid of the pigs?"

"Uluru, what are you so worried about? A circus is coming into this town soon. Then you can sell the monkeys to the circus at a bargain price."

"Oh! That'll do it."

Uluru was still looking at his mother when he said that. Originally, it was because the owner of the farm was a mother. This was because Uluru has run the farm after she had Alzheimer's. Nevertheless, his innermost thoughts have already decided to sell of the farm. Notifying mom was a matter afterwards. It had to avoid the fever without suffering any major damage right now. The group's memory was very simple. Simplicity went too far and so far as to be foolish.

Everyone has been brainwashed by fever. It never seemed to have been so quiet that night. It has been a few more days since that night. Still, all she could do was sit in a rocking chair and stare out the window all day long, except for sleeping. At the slaughterhouse, dozens of kilometers from the village, they were looking for pigs to use for meat before the fever hit the village.

The wholesalers first came to Uluru's house. It was early in the morning. Before breakfast, they parked a pickup truck in the yard of house and called Uluru out, knocking hard at the creaking gate with their palms.

"Who the hell is this morning? I couldn't even eat breakfast."

"Oh, I'm sorry. We are wholesalers who have come to buy pigs. Soon enough, this place won't be safe from swine fever, so I hope you can sell it to us before that, but we can pay the price enough."

Uluru's wife, attracted by his words, pecked at his side and whispered something in his ear.

"Honey, I want you to ask how much you want to buy it."

Uluru thought of something for a moment and then opened his mouth.

"How much do you want to buy our pigs?"

"I'll give you $200 per."

That was a good price. It was important for Uluru to sell them before they all died of fever. He began to bargain again.

"How about $250?"

"Well, I'll give you up to $220."

"Good. Take it for $220 per."

"I'd like to take the pigs right now, would you mind?"

"Of course. Take them all."

After the word was finished, I led them into the place where the pigs were gathered. Counting one by one, there were 157. They all paid in bills and handed them over to me. The total was $34,500. I thought I should take this money rather than lose it all in a fever. They brought some big trucks in the afternoon and began to load one at a time.

Damn wholesalers, they were sure to slaughter all the pigs to make meat and sell them for $100 a kilogram. However, it was inevitable.

It was obvious that failure to do so would result in massive damage due to the pig fever.

Everything was suddenly decided and settled. It felt as if one of my long-suffering cavities had been missing.

Uluru and his wife breathed a sigh of relief at least for selling the pigs quickly; counting the money, they had received at one time. Now I have solved the scourge of swine fever. All that remains is to sell off the house, which was born and raised, and leave here. The idea of raising a pig is gone. For the next few years, this country will be swept away like a plague because of fever.

Wholesalers loaded all the pigs on the farm into trucks.

Some pigs struggled not to get on the truck, as if they knew their fate for the future. Some pigs were even caught running away. With a whip, one at a time all loaded onto the truck and left the farm. Trucks began to drift away from Uluru's view. Chuck and his flock were riding in the back seat of the last truck. Then a circus troupe had already arrived in the town square and a bugle was heard to mark the start of the circus.

The end

the eve of the revolution

1.

One night they left,
the last plane to the Europe in July
did not come back to where they landed.
The remnants are still far from spring,
but they can remember.
This place we live in is still waiting for
those who will return,
There will be another life there.
The red halo is still weeping
in that mountain range.
With our dirty hands still unwashing of
all the revolutions in the past,
we must take the next plane
that will not be delayed.
The things that are still available
to us are those that can bear
in the wide wing,

2.

Is it time for the sun to rise again on that wing?
Do we have to leave this place with
whom we are with you today?

The small birds that grow on the small
leaves are forgotten in their ears.
Red Square hid the rainwater flowing all night.
The clock tower in the square will indicate the time
to go to the new site.
We remember that time.
Our little comrades!
Try to play the piano keys on untuned streets.
Let's meet on this wing when dawn comes.
Our lives will never be delayed.
Just as you cannot stop time,
you cannot stop the future of growing birds,

Song of a revolutionary

1.

Have you ever forgotten the night of March
that year when the moonlight always sat
on a dry branch over the window
and did not come down from there all night?
The sound of a cricket that forgot the seasons
knocked on the window all night
and the sound would call like my name,
and I would have lonely alone at dawn.
I saw the broken barrier around the yard.
I was afraid to cross the border every day,
so I did not open the window in the morning.
The wreckage of cold frosts gradually
penetrating into the underground,
the painful time makes it an unknown believer,
and the memories of last night's horror bring pride
and vain conviction.
The day will come when no one will come.
Then I will see the blackened space again,
and the fading fallen down by the ever smaller sound. Have
you ever forgotten the night with the old flag and the little cry?
Absolute solitude that cannot wait for
anyone anymore!

2.

Where do you come from?
There is a place where the water does not dry
in the summer, unstoppable land, wildflowers are full, and
your footprint is clear in my sight.
Last spring, the hummingbird,
who stopped by for a while,
grows up all the time and spends plenty of honey.
The flowing time is also beautiful.
I will remember the young face of
my dispersed comrades.
When you leave a clear footprint to
where you came from,
the stars will follow the path.
Some poor and dreamy little girls will come with me. Stars
pouring out tonight call the wind.
Warm wind blows in my ear.
Loneliness does not fall in a spawning heart;
no one can stay in a space that cannot rest.
Their names fade away from their ears
and the boys who cannot grow up still stand
at the entrance to the village,
and his broken screams resemble
the sound of our songs that do not stop.

Old man

Have you ever looked at the moonlight in this city?
Old man,
winds blowing through the pink buildings
they cannot stay this winter night.
The streetlight resembles the broken space ship
that dreamed of being a child from a Milky Way.
They have to dance and play
on the sidewalk block that will not stop.
Everyone is laughing.
Only the puppy who lost his master keeps
the last without leaving.
The dry thunder is not so amazing.
I hear the cries of those birds
that have not stepped on the dry land
in the underground river flowing through the city.
I remember the name of the knights
who left for the forest a long time ago.
Where they vanished,
I could touch the wind.
Cannot you see?
There to see the silver sunshine.

Friendly...

Blue Moon

1.

Blue Moon,
I went to school for my childhood,
which turned into ruins.
The fragments of shattered memory
are constantly making my past work.
Last time, the ginkgo trees of the campus
that have been preserved here do not grow up
as they did not grow up.
Where the friends of my childhood
who met me see where the pain is now,
the blue moon and stars that floats
above the mountains before the sun goes down,
the long time when they unfold like a floodlight,
the thoughts that have been entangled with
the flourishes that have grown up all the time.
This is always a hard workshop in my life.
When I turn on the light again
and replace the darkness,
I will be decorated with flowers
in this ruined place.
As my nostalgic friends,

2.

Where did the strength of the hidden shells
hiding and the strength of the mountains
that had changed over the countless years
and changed the lives of those who had been so painful?
When I realized the point of view
that there is no eternal longing,
I could only see the old piece of chalk hardened into ruins
and fallen in the pulpit.
The dry monsoon and lightning frustration
on the mountain ridge
that does not fall to the ground
sometimes shines on it.
This city cannot accommodate many crosses.
Every night we go up on the garden
and write down the obituary of those who
went up to heaven that night.
Do not forget this place.
I see a group of minnows living in a small puddle.
They know that.
A sad sound on a quiet land.
Their crying cries on the cross
that they cannot leave even when they leave.

3.

Shadows,

in the sinking the ever - lasting imagination
of the world, always tranquil we had to cross
the last train to the end of Europe at midnight.
There was no one on top of the summit,
breathless.
We waited for someone on the platform.
But it sounds like the sound of the dead men
heading home, in the shadow,
in despair with the imagination
that we can always meet this dawn for a long night, we've been
holding the railing of the continents to the end.
The night cannot beat the dawn.
Dawn cannot overcome despair again.
We always repeat trips to the land every day.

the daffodils of April

1.

In one of the poor painters' chambers,
his splendid days, which he had never met before,
were being painted on the canvas.
The daffodils of April never faded.
He saw a time of young youth
who did not grow old or sad.
By the railroad track that is not always rusty,
the future children are gathering
and watching the stars in the night sky.
It would be a memory for the life that was in it.
The wind collects in one place and comforts
those who have to live with a passion.
People there! Flowers, our beautiful gardens!
Do not stay with the faded pictures in the drawers.
The fragments of nostalgia are attached to each other. The
precious moments that
he had with the memories of the painful days
came together in love with longing.

2.

Everything that stands on the hill has no fault,

no matter where I put it.
It will always resemble its humility.
The white snow-covered mountains
and the small seeds have now come to know
that there are so many of the deer
that resemble our traces, resembling us.
When I walked along the long riverbank,
there was always a railroad track to go to a place
where we wanted to go.
The zelkova in front of the town
where we rode with our younger companions
was still a big tree for us.
The old houses that lived together
were on the hill.
The song,
which the children sang along the stonewall together,
must be alive in our deep breath.
Now spring is coming soon.
A lovely time will come,
resembling the shy child,

clowns

In the fearsome heat that has come in decades
The weak have made the weaker
and the poor to fall into hell.
Someone told me.
As long as the fireballs deep in your heart
do not cool down
Fear will come from contention and death,
Ultimately,
divide the beautiful feelings of
all those living and breathing,
I will not let you go to the place
I have been searching for,
I will go quietly, threaten, and ridicule it,
Our clowns are gone,
that this land is no longer a stage,
He said he would teach me soon.
Hot heat will evaporate our innocence.
Behold the drift of those things
that have lost their emotions,
The spirit of spring,
The death of the berries to be cooked red
in summer.
I could not prepare anything at the time.
Brown harvest and
I lost the silent thought of the snow - covered earth.
From the pilgrims who went to the east,

I could not receive a letter for that year.
These empty memories,
Souls of the earth who are in a starving spirit,

robin

Was it an early winter morning with frost?
I walked along the foggy forest path
to a small lake.
Already the surface of the lake
was covered with thin ice.
The frost was sitting on top of it.
The footprint of one of the little robins
was pinned tightly over it toward
the center of the lake.
My eyes face the middle of the lake along
the trail of three branches.
My feelings were also searching for
traces of a small bird in late fall,
which I grew up walking along a forest.
The mist in the forest has not faded away
and the air pressure accumulated early
in the morning wakes up all living things.
Last summer people raised a hue
and cry about the drying up of the land.
There was not the slightest regret
at the site of the fever.
They were not qualified to stroll
through this forest.
The traces of that little creature could not follow.
Pride and selfish spirits will soon fall asleep

under the weight of this fog,
and will become a treasure of the laughter
and verbosity of the salmon running back
a small valley each year.
I will always be small.
This lightness is fun.
I have to walk lightly to the center of the lake,
where it is hidden by dense fog
and I do not know what there is.

path, on any road

1.

Just as anything breaks easily according to clouds,
Falling down also follows established rules.
Spreading the alignment of time and space
In a crack that we have not seen in our home
It is preparing for the terrible time for all the collapse.
As the course of the coming storm
and its weight cannot be measured
How should I meet these suddenly inevitable times?
In the march of myriad pilgrims
As no one can predict
what steps will become true guides
When the light of the lighthouse is blurred
The dark seas have long voyages, losing the mark.
Someday, this little space where we stand
It will collapse according to clouds.
Where are you going to be trapped
in the sharpest and narrowest space?
Yet the end of the wind is not so cold
Before the waves are over,
before everything sinks
We must end this harsh and holy path.

2.

On any road

I confess that it is the most blessed way
to walk with someone who loves,
especially looking at the rising sun
through the thin clouds.
Today we sent to heaven a saint
who has a sincere heart like a shepherd
who was poor but lived honestly with anyone.
Thinking about those times
that were beautiful to anyone
We also know that when we leave things
that we have always held and leave
How pleasant it is.
I confess that he is a teacher
and lover of life.
Where is a gentle slope?
A person who is beautiful,
I always walk in the happiest memory,
thinking of only the flowering.
There is no quarrel.
A greed is like a steam that will easily disappear,
On this road or on any cobbled road
If you confess that, you are not sad,

mirage

I saw a mirage on the way back.
A stranger approaches, speaks,
and promises that I cannot keep.
I will contact you again.
I will write if necessary.
I did not enjoy friendliness.
Again, you experience the drift of language.
Someday this road will be over.
At that time,
you will not see a mirage from a distance.
One or two must leave this room.
I split the unit of time
and listen to the sound of bumping into each other.
It is no stranger anymore.
Our neural networks come together like friends
and hang out.
I will contact you again.
No, I will not confirm.
Maybe even the friendliness
we have waited there will be a mirage.
Anyone can be welcomed.
A small change covers the city like a mist.
Even if the pressure fails
and the moments of joy collapse
I also wanted to make everyone happy.

It will look like a mirage
on the way back from far away.

I'm dreaming of a revolution.

One summer night,
beautiful sound flows
in the entrance of the village.
The moonlight is red,
and sometimes the cuckoo
in the forest does not sleep,
singing to the sound.
I followed the sound
and found a house with a small lamp lit.
In our small yard where we missed everybody,
There were some nice people
who seemed to meet sometime and danced.
The sound of the winds of the summer night
and the nostalgic family
And friends who did not grow up were beautiful.
I look for myself.
In the low place,
I sang a song with a drink of wine
that somebody would pour in my cup.
I was really blessed in my childhood.
If this time has not left my mood with
that moonlight,
The life of the garden!
If I sing together and drink the wine all night
and put embroidery on the night sky,

I will find the time of youth bound in love.
After waking up from a long sleep,
if I knew that it was a place of golden gorgeous youth

pieces of memory and a child

Pieces of memory
With the memories of the painful season
when we came back to our space
We will have to leave the strangers.
The space is struggling to support
a collapsed wall
that no one comes to.
In front of the rain that summer night
The dampness of the damp from the deep in the earth,
awakened by the sad cry of the scattered,
The leaves that survive the dying
and survive the harsh drought do not lose
their color,
If you gave me that life,
That this road like the desert was never lonely,
The pieces of memory that raised without notice
In front of their madness
We must always meet the late season.
We saw a water strider walking on
a polluted surface.
It is the place of their tryst,
We hear a blunt sound.
One night in a tranquil temple,
After the storm of the summer,
There we will meet a boy who collects sculptures.

We will meet innocent youth
who cross the desert without water.
We will not always be forgotten in the seasons,
This land will have glorious days
that we have never known,
The wind will go away,
and the sound of the flute of the child will be heard,

my lamp

1.

Please remove that lamp
whose light inside is turned off.
No one will come to you tonight.
There are guests lying on the deep river floor.
I cannot hear the camel's crying,
and in the autumn night,
we will hear a cricket sound in the grass.
At that time,
I hope you do not think to avoid darkness
along the dark mountain road.
I just hope that the lamp will turn on again.
A messenger spoke.
The sound of the wind cannot be heard.
Still, the city's wetlands do not forsake hope.
Look at the feast of small flames on the wick.
Imagine the seasons of blooming on a small hill.
Please find my lamp's light.
Then the guys who lost their memories
on there will see the day
when their childhood dreams
will come alive again.

2.

There's no reason for the wall to fall.
It will probably do it because no one comes
or misses someone.
The struggle of the little birds
that have lost their nests will miss the wick of the ramp.
Whenever this void disappears,
it will be the day when some small light
among the dense stones will sound silently.
A small gathering on the side of the road
will be a pleasure of a rich dining table.
Then the little mountain will be greener,
the river will be deep and beautiful
and serene, my lamp!
Come back and light up the fire.

the man

1.

It was like an embarrassed excuse.
The castrated cats fell asleep on the shelf,
and the fallen cottages were
the only complaints of a long queue.
For what purpose do we have to keep this old city
that all of us have left tonight?
We remember that night that was gorgeous.
The days when the excuses of
those who lost a mate were
as beautiful as the cover of a childish magazine
that even tears.
We see the back of the man
who went into the deep mountain to build poetry.
The man who left countless excuses like
dust is probably our lost noble form.

2.

I see a picture in the background of a sea in the wall.
When the boundaries between the walls
and the sea were gone,
I saw an elderly man walking out of the picture.

He was no longer the weak.
Refusing the rank,
the boundary was pushed to the depths
of the coast by the waves.
I grew up to be a mature adult
and met people who stand with the wall
and shared a long story.
There is a moon in the night sky;
it always shines on the sea.
There are no boundaries,
so we cannot see the weak of the land anymore.

a forest way

1.

Memory makes another season
and a way that no one has walked in a forest
that has never walked.
Behold,
the calm words that permeates through the leaves,
the morning will come beautifully in every season of our lives,
and I will be the season for them.
There is a sound from small waterfall in the land
we wanted to see,
in our memories there is a school of our childhood,
a small hut,
and a school of cloisters dressed with ivy vines
that have few students.
Remember,
there is a place that is not forgotten
among the neighbors who call other seasons
and give warmth and greetings at any time.

2.

I see the history of old colonies at this grave.
I see a square tube and a colored corolla on it.

An old monument that nobody
cares about tells me to take off the chain.
You were the hero of history.
No, you were just a guest on a quiet earth.
All of us have lived differently
in the brittle history of colonialism,
and we only want to get out of this bridle
under the same sky last time together
with the wonderful corolla of the square.
There probably will not be a wind.
So you cannot see the flowers
that bloom in the spring.
The era of colonization will not be spring.
Is the night of colonization dark?
The wind is sleeping
and the full moon is a bright night.

commotion

There was a commotion in a small village.
Rioters that cannot be ignored never piled up
on the streets during the night of snow.
That night, no familiar drunken man could hear
the song again.
It was not that deep at night
and I could not find people.
Just inadvertently,
too much time is tied under dim mercury lamppost,
waiting for dawn to come.
At midnight,
buses that do not pick up passengers
are hit by falling snow from the night sky,
turning around the corner,
and only cats, who will live like the king of the night,
call their mates with unending cries.

the coastline

1.

The gray skies above the coastline,
the border, are pouring water
and then breathing. There is no gray fence.
The lost ocean current suffers from pneumonia
in the distant sea.
When the horizon crosses
the boundary like a fence,
we will have to wait for humpback whales,
taking a deep breath
and going on a trip to the deep sea
beyond this fence, seeing the sun sinking.
It was our face breathing
in the deep red sea,
resembling the old man's face.

2.

I see cutlass fish that have climbed from
the deep sea to the shore,
and I see fear in the eyes of villagers
living on the sea sinking down like darkness.
It was no longer the appearance of

those who survived the war in solidarity.
Deep under the sea, hollow shell washed up by the sea
and the waves began to control the thoughts
and words of the continental strangers
in the land to which the owner changed.
I had hoped long ago
that this sea could be a small hill
with easy-to-climb trees.
That was not my idea.
I would follow that long ago
when I could have gotten the idea of going
to the sea from an elk or roots
that got lost in the woods
and rotten raspberries from the roots.
The waves danced more violently.
From then on,
every time they saw an unknown creature
that climbed from the deep sea and died,
the villages of the territory began to disappear
one by one.

3.

I knew the blue sea,
the names on the sand dunes
that were not erased for a long time,
the wind blowing in the East.
At any given time,

I go to the place where my memories dancing,
where the stories of the mammals
that came from the land rising on the big water hills are
engraved. Waiting for the time
that the land will be connected
Waiting for the moon to light
the dark night sea to rise above that mountain.
I will miss the days of the red aged rather than
the blue youth,
and the sea will soon boil up.
Our days are brilliantly beautiful.

roadkill

1.

I watched a wild deer killed by a car
driving on Route 1.
 The creature of the forest,
picking the last breath at the end of a long tire trace,
was the scene of a memory of dreams
that I had seen at some time.
I imagined the future of our land on the road
where the fog started,
holding a ritual in the forest
where I had lifted its body
as if it was asleep quietly.
Songs flow out among the tree branches.
The young birch lost its voices
throughout the winter,
and at the end of February,
it wanted to reap the wreck of the forest
and bring a warm aura.
Silence does not suit the season.
Old leaves falling down
against the branches of trees,
I am still treading the leaves for listening the weep,

2.

Who were we looking for
with the long procession of dead,
the images of funerals,
the sounds of a garden filled with moisture
and the cries of a bishop?
The only festival
that lost the joy of being overshadowed
by the spell of strangers
who were rescued from the village of silence.
No one wanted to go down the path of rough gravel.
The only ones whose purpose is
unknown were those who did not know.

3.

The mind is distracted
and the way to go this evening is far.
The darkness does not show the road already,
but the cuckoo that cannot find the nest is ungainly
and it is a common routine to homeless on the road.
In the light of the moon,
the clouds are flowing,
and finding the way ahead.
Have you ever felt such cold frost in the night?
Behind the hill leaping lightly,
my dear home will greet me.

pieces of revolution

1.

Puzzles of memorized pieces
in one night dream,
when waking up from a long sleep,
I penetrate into the unconscious again.
Looking at my familiar self
as I look out of the opaque window
as if I come back from a dreamlike walk.
This was a piece that was
well fitted to the shadows of people
who looked at the distant outskirts
of a strange neighborhood.
I am now jealous.
On a dead end street,
I see a different road.
A bright day will come.
The day will come when
I will shed tears to make you dazzle.
My pieces do not sleep until then.
The morning of the bright memory!
The dead are alive in that park.

2.

The refractions of the sound falling
on the branches,
the sob of those who have long
since left the earth.
The sighs of fishermen
who were polishing old fishing nets
and the wreckage
that crashed into the deep waters,
some crying was the sob of the dolphins trapped
in the aquarium.
This place is more like a sea
before it was created.
Today I see the brothers in their sweet days.

3.

Unknown poets all of the little insects
in the grass that did not wake up
to sleep were memories of a summer night.
In that month,
the full moon was covered in the clouds,
and only a deep breathing wind was heard.
It was a dark cloud that lasted for several days.
One day,
while waiting for these memories
to come back to their place,

the poet made a will for the world people
in a blank piece of paper
that would not be filled at night.

glaciers

1.

This is still the age of glaciers.
The frozen earth covered all our memories.
The end of the road
covered with snow was not seen,
and the ancient traces locked in a glacier
where the remainder of the horses
were lost were kept unchanged.
Where did their dreams begin?
Where the glacier melts
and where it comes from,
the crying ceases and the blizzard is still here,

2.

I am walking through the season of a thaw
that will someday be back,
the sea of memories I have missed and frozen.
I am looking at the fields of polar bears
and white wolves who lost their mother back from land.
Spores of seeds hid in deep grounds
without the appearance of a brilliant warrior
must have been rich meadows;

there were only sad stories of frozen emotions
and aboriginal people returning to their vulgar world.

them or them

1.

This was a road
that had not yet been completed
and had never been.
How many of those huge cogs are waving here?
You see creatures that cannot sleep deeply,
other hidden Earth's mountains that cannot climb.
Pilgrims on the mountain path.
They are not coming back.
I could not despair.
Those who crave their names,
the shadows that resemble
the beasts of the mountains.
We cannot drift on the frozen sea.
Nothing more than the meaningless characters
in literature that crumble in it.

2.

The scattered characters
were put together again.
There is another lost civilization
in the place that could not leave.

Perhaps it would have been
their language to take off satellites
that would not be returned to a certain star
by densely packed cogs,
but we will not forget the words.
Poets and novelists
who left the land a long time ago
from which star are they writing letters
to the strange earth.
Their hearts were not cold.
In this frozen ground,

seasonal street

1.

The birds flying to the end of any mountain,
deep, did not come back.
They saw the railroad that followed
the two mountains.
The traces of coal that has been shed long
before the rusty railroad will not be lost here.
The day will run again.
Mahogany workers,
those who moved to the frozen ground,
did not return.
The mountain is always like that,
our long breath rusts,

2.

Where it started on the road
to a homely house,
nobody taught people who met on this way.
However,
the sincerity of the birds flying over
the fence could not bear the burden of
the stranger on the front door of any house.

The poverty separated us so that
the rich memories would now remain
as vain thoughts,
and the festival of thanksgiving
was held on the seasonal streets of the old homeless.
It will not be anywhere in any part of the world,
but this desolate land was the dust
and the wind of the sand,
and the vain fog from the west.

old gardens

1.

Old gardens,
like the hands of somebody,
familiar stone sculptures,
and pictures of those children
who have not arrived yet,
figures in the walls spray-painted somewhere;
still our heart is snowy winter.
Today, we decided to meet folk at that time.
They are the promised traces.
The train to depart from midnight
will not be delayed anymore.
Even if the snow is piled up
and the children do not come,
it is always a garden that will not fall down.

2.

Its pieces of mind that are irreconcilable.
Strangers who forget their senses,
children who have lost their words,
babies who cannot grow up,
old people who can't go back to their nest,

have remembered a well in the middle of the desert
somewhere.
I came to an empty library today.
Where there was no one,
where there was no one to borrow books
or lend them, winter in the desert,
in the spirit of my ancestor,
there was an inexhaustible well.
It was the winter of life
when it was the last to cry.

3.

In the spring, the haze will bloom.
With the morning sun shining brightly,
along with those who climb up
the mountain with breathlessness,
in the minds of those who have to choose
on the two divided paths,
they must abandon the excitement of the new day
and the lingering fuss about
the beautiful northern winds
there will always be people waiting for us.
In these trivial times in this desolate village,

4.

Children's memories are locked,
the laughter of the young ladies seeping
around the stone walls,
the landscape that did not subside for joy
and their sighing sound
under the long winter night's horror light,
now we have to hide inside the morning haze.
Nothing has happened,
and you should keep rumors
about the day to those passing by.
The names of the comrades
and the long lengthening
that they left must be buried in a well
where the stars are sleeping
and the moon is dancing.

Gastown, the street of revolution

1.

Gastown,
city where the light does not fall,
on the red carpet,
some sleeping,
the streets where it does not freeze,
the flaming sun is rising over the sea
between a young John singing a flute
and a puppy,
Someday when the steam rising
on the surface of the water points to midnight,
there will be only the laughter
of the dancers and singers,
the Gentiles from faraway countries
and children who will come forward
with dreams of the future,
Oh, my spirit that will not forget!
The rubious sun that will rise from Deep Ocean!

2.

Horizon,
the place where we can see the boundaries,

which way to go there will not have to wander again,
Compass of companions
who lost friends and passengers under the moon,
we go on a long journey in caravan over midnight.
Somewhere,
even if they pass through a dry valley,
you will find a deep fountain
that somebody has uncovered,
and they will know that it is beautiful
and mild on there.

3.

When you look at the barren path
that anyone can take right of this unruly spirit,
and wait for this old garden to bloom,
you see the strange lovers
who broke up here one day,
and I remember that the wind's end was not so cold,
and the bugle of revolution is still ringing in my ears,
and the moon
that I see today is not the light of its shape
and in darkness,
Is the sound of those who tread
on the ground of the garden so intimate?

4.

The hot southerly wind continues to blow,
but trunk cannot go anywhere,
this is still a glacier island
where everything has frozen,
a long forgotten episode,
a small squirrel which has lost way through the forest,
a frost that has not melted overnight,
One tree covered with dry leaves
and a heart that avoids the cold;
That's how life is going!
What did you leave out
and how did you cry out in the world?
Young poet!
Your heart is always alive in the southern wind,

5.

When the most precious things were leaving
one by one, the Midnight Train,
which sought to calm the mind,
kept the spot without leaving the old platform.
At that time,
we scratched the rusty of all things
on the rusty rails
and we waited there at dawn every night.

6.

The unknown poems
and their cries,
the last dinner of the poor,
and the snowflake that ran hard that winter,
stood on the streets that season.
In the winter of thought,
the selfish criticism of the narrowed ones
and their binge eaters were ordered to them.
There will always be a seat at the edge of it.
Wherever you are, do not return.
A silent revolution did not end up
like a vulgar stone on the roadside.

7.

To live on the feet of the earth
means to endure the dirt,
dust and ooze blowing from the west;
our forests still do not sleep.
Could it be that the spring is not warm?
In a deceased world, early folly is tossed.
And when you leave a way alone,
things like the territory are dirty
and you just throw them away.
I see a small bird flying freely.

8.

I walked the streets paved with red bricks
I saw the faces that passed by,
I looked back with my eyes
and soul like the one I met at some time.
There I see only the back of many people,
and the face that I have seen is disappearing into
the back of everyone.
What planet has this fallen from?
What is this meteor shower?
I ride children's broken spaceship
and need to find my face again vanishing back into
a dream among the lonely crowd.

9.

I did not even know
that my shoes were dirty
and I was standing on the mud.
But I cannot take off my shoes.
I have to accept the remnants of filth
that come up to my heart as mine.
The lilies on the mud are beautiful all the time;
I cannot even make that flower,
if all things on earth were standing like that,

10.

There is a shadow
that waits so long.
Everything was right there.
Things that will disappear
leaving a long lasting day,
things that cannot catch anything it was a shadow.
It was a shadow to tempt me to come around
and hop.

dream

1.

We think of a ship that flies mainly
to the deeply space,
now there is a to be left in this humanity
where there is no one who
is flying along the boundaries of the universe.
We must lay the bridge in the night sky
that shines bright tonight.
We should not break the dream of
the young man who slept a stone pillow.
When this place is wide open,
it will send a pretty picture of ours
on their faraway ships,

2.

Today we must miss someone.
Waiting for the train to leave the empty station.
Maybe the old fog that last night did not disappear.
To be able to recognize a dim shape in it,
I have to prepare for a story to share
with the flowing times sitting on
a bench commemorating someone with a friend,

who can know everything and know me first,

3.

Meet the ears of those who hide in the wall,
the whispers of those who are coming from
outside the window at dawn,
and the shadows that come behind the long sundown,
and tell us our stories.
It was the cries of the people who belonged to it was.
On unpaved roads,
anyone is left with a long footprint,
a trail to which point they should follow today,
a place where the stars disappear,
along the old walls of a place where they crumble.

painters

1.

Poor painters poured into the streets.
In cold weather,
they painted the city with hardened paint
and old brushes.
Silence began at the end of their hands,
and the city was reborn as a revolution of color.
Tamed doves by urban life will not leave here.
Where color cannot be discerned,
people will boast about the color of their lies.
Everyone is color blind.
Just like a nude that does not bother anything,
a painter who has lost a soul
and a deadly loophole make it color-blind
by drawing their own colors.

2.

Spring,
someday when we will all fade away
by the end of the season,
then it will be the only cold chill.
All the beasts of the prairies

will then leave here in search of a warm aura.
Where are we in the seasons
when we can no longer find the atmosphere
to be covered with dust,
the flock of goats to go to the highest places on earth,
and the flowers of our garden.

3.

  If I see the world with the bird's eyes,
I will not be there,
because there is no place
to fold a shameful heart.
When we think of an old friend
who flew into the land of Eastern frozen Siberia,
there will be memories of us in their eyes,
the train is delayed,
and the beloved do not come.
If we sing to the world with a bird's mouth,
we will not be there to dance to the rhythm.

4.

A town isolated by heavy rains,
broken bridges, cats that lost their masters,
the nightfall of the sloping mountain streams,
the walkways have crumbled

and they have lost their way,
and this city has seen such a collapse,
The misinformation
and thorough alienation flow down the wet buildings,
the sorrows and cries of those who have lost their masters,
the wet tents must be rolled,
the distinction of the land
where the stones of the unnamed people
and the stones of the old are built up,
Looking at the isolated temple,
seeing the collapse of the wandering people.

5.

sparrows and bustling,
the cuckoos and magpies,
and our hummingbirds
The names of the flowers
and the faces of the passing away
are buried untouched,
and their little songs revolves around us,
like ours that resemble
the waves of a small cobblestone
thrown on the lake memories
will call us from somewhere beyond,

change of season

The change of seasons resembles
the boundary of the mind.
During the turn of the seasons,
the universe will lose its guard
and drift away.
The glorious days of a distant empire
can no longer be expected of everlasting,
for those who have enjoyed
their rich days cannot be found.
Which border are we looking at now?
We will send hearts across
the Continent of Repentance to see
the migratory birds who have just learned to fly away.

delusion of reed

1.

The reed forests rooted in dry land,
the sound of the bumps,
the deep stories of the nesting shorebirds.
Their roots will miss the mud drenched
in a deep breeze.
When the dry wind passes,
and someday they have to leave here,
the whispering swinging reed resembles their crying.
When the river rises there again,
Oh! That day was a day of their bright,
memories of prosperity,

2.

There is no reason to get out of delusion.
Waiting for the mist of this morning to be lifted,
I watch the parade going to the workplace early
in the daybreak.
Some of them will knock the frozen land
late at night and awaken the unconscious of
those who are sleeping quietly.
It is not strange for them to have no light.

Everything goes toward the end.
The sunshine is scarce,
and the delusions that float
in time climb over the heavily packed plaid streets
by sleeping one by one.

3.

Cracked ice walls,
breathing sounds that rise again every thousand years,
yet there are indelible shouts and footprints,
and where no one will disappear,
a small seed will be raised from a hiding place,
so this tough life and our trail will breathe.

standing on the boundary

1.

Those who have the boundary
between holiness and deceit,
and those who are too pure to measure their distance.
A premature infant who does not know
who their mother is takes a breath in the corner of the street.
For those who are on border,
and who will follow them into an endless abyss,
always have no idea which side to stand on

2.

The buried ones, and the long silence,
the fixed seasons that come back and forth,
the familiar faces that rise,
the names of the poor writers,
the birds on the banks of the river,
and the long funeral processions endlessly end.
I have never been brave before.
When I saw their shadows that would be taken away,
I became a shadow trapped in the grey building
so that no one would hear it.
Someone shouted,

Our revolution was crazy,
we waved flags on the red building,
but the people who walked down the street
became plaster, as if they had never seen it,
and the snows that fell on the hard road covered the clear
bloodstains of the street.
I have never been brave there.
I have never been on the street.
I just stared silently through the misty window.

the land of resistance

1.

In the land of resistance,
the cat on the street is also scared.
The dream of rebellion will be growing
in their hearts that are quietly approaching.
Their language,
which has long been exploited and castrated,
has increasingly begun to acquire human speech.
The revolutionary army of the earth
that waited so long did not come,
and when the fears and tremors about
the trivial things spread like
an anesthetic shot into the whole body,
it began to show some sort of respect for those
which met in the street.
A situation tamed them.
The hidden instinct was covered with
a soft colored fabric.
Long boots were not visible,
but only the last fallen leaves of the season,
which had been crushed helplessly under the feet,
were wrapped around their ankles.
They might have envied the old settlers
who once walked on two feet

and contemplated them.
Now it is no longer necessary.
This is because the stone altar
that no one could touch and destroy are piled up.
On top of it,
the Milky Way of the Night sky comes down
and puts a ceremony.
Seriousness and piety are also tamed.

2.

I could not hate him.
Early dawned guests knocking on the door,
I knew I could not be forgotten.
The stones thrown at them will never make waves.
We must follow the sacrifice of a young noble man.
We must shed a tear while looking at the back of the one who
carries holiness and belonging together.
The praise of the blessed, the comfort of the poor,
the pangs of the angry, the rest of the weary,
and the breath of life.
Today,
the night scenery of one of the rural villages
is unusually brightened by the stellar stars in the sky.

3.

The wanderers,
the barren sand hills
and the traces of a brief stay by us wandering
through the storm,
the hope for Oasis waited for the scattered cloud to come
together. It was not a short life.
There was always an old map of a world
that had been hidden beyond the horizon in its pockets.
When this hill changes again and becomes a beach,
a small bottle of our walkway is washed away,
and we will stay with the welcoming
and forgotten of those who crave innocence
and build a castle together.
The sound of dust and wind scattered through the air,
and breaths and clear springs flowed.

missing

The little grasshopper's delicate sound
makes the autumn nightfall deeper into silence.
There is a blessing to think more,
and before this night is over,
we shall have some enlightenment.
The deep sound of the earth shaking millions of years ago
has not yet been woken up,
and all the precious things we have seen in space are waiting
for us in the deep earth.
When can we go there,
take out the faded paper,
and count the promises one by one?
Everywhere, anywhere was poor,
but tomorrow I will always think of
when I was thrilled with waiting.
The end of the wind from there will never be cold,
so you will wake up from your deep sleep
and climb up the hill where the reeds shake.
The front side of discrimination is solitude,
the forest road without speculation goes into
a maze without exit, two walkers who forget their names
and walk silently,
and Deep underground is now trying to tell the secret.
Our wells have begun to dry from now on,
that we will not come again to water here again;

there we must hear the cries of wild birds
that their wings have broken.
The cry is like the voice of an orphan.
It resembles the story of a ginkgo
that did not grow up in front of the wasteland.
It was a farmer's cry over the ruins of a rural village
where one or two left.
I have to listen to the story of a child who was born
without knowing words affluence.
The land has never fallen,
but this place has become where stand up cannot again,
where we cannot go into orbit,
where can only live if we miss the past.

Behind the Moon

The old stories heard on Moai Island,
the lost language in the letters of
those who could not leave the land a long time ago became
stars in any universe.
The flock of eagles flying over the border
and the swarm of salmon that could not return to the
spawning grounds,
the children who could not remember them
and the town could not have everyone.
The frequent funeral procession
and the increasing cries of eagles were seen
in the mountain village where the cries of newborn babies
were no longer heard.
The only consolation was the firm conviction
that protected them.
I could not see the broken tracks
and the people trying to get to the peak.
I was looking for a footprint in the middle of the desert,
amidst the grief of the lost.
Where the image of the fossilized men was built,
there is nothing left behind their shadows,
Can we return to the back of the memory we have been
waiting for?
The Isle no longer spoke,
no more news in the wind,

in a desolate place,
where one has to miss.
We had to wait for it beyond the horizon
we were looking at,
an unfinished dry rainy season.
The waves did not rush to the beach,
just laying down the dead
and being washed down into the distant ocean,
our thoughts wandered beyond the horizon,
and we have to go where no one could expect them.
Standing on the back of the earth
at the sound of the waves,
hoping that someone would call their forgotten name.

Standing on the sundown hill,

I watch the wild flower beneath my feet,
lifting up its slender body to see everything in the world.
Have you heard their breaths
and their invincible vitality?
Even at night,
it will not bend over to get into its nest.
The air is no longer a narrow place.
The windage cannot shake its body,
so it will not fall anywhere.
It will not be silent in the rain
or wind anymore.
Nothing to be forgotten,
I wait for the souls of those who have crossed the fence into
the forbidden land.
Then we have to wait for the guests from another land,
so we will wake up the frozen lake
and realize that every moment we have to live
when it is warm again is not a burden.
When I realized that this was not a shabby place
that I could not live with,
there was no one left around.
I must miss something again.
I have no place to go on the ground
I have to listen to the faded leaves
and hear the sad story.

It is the time to close the doors on the ground.
Their shadows sleep between day and night.

the death of an actress

The sun does not set on the red sorghum field.
On the last way of an old actress,
we have to wait for someone.
In the passion of unknown actors
and nameless writers,
who will not yet come,
who will put down their soul,
the streets will not be frozen with their breath
and the heart of cold days.
Call out a name that is floating somewhere
on this street.
On a day when the city in wetlands were glorious,
we should wait to hear the applause of the unknown audience,
the heartless resignation song,
and the dance trapped in the shadows.
Every passing thing is meant to be,
but it is nothing to disappear with.
Those that break down in the waves of the beach,
those that will not return,
are the memories of the good old days,
and those who miss will go,
and where the wind stays on the hill,
will only leave traces of the sparrow.
By the time the parade of the long picnic is over,
now we must sit face to face with the end of

all the stories.
We must open the door for the soul that waits,
at any time our spring day will be.
Despair is also a sumptuosity;
looked at the river running on the broken bridge.
The fragment that breaks down on a wobbly skeleton,
she may be missing some glorious days in such another world.

some wandering

No one waits on the mudflat.
I have long forgotten my time here.
I want to hear the story of a shell
without any feet that came up into
this space after wandering
thousands of kilometers under the sea.
This is not the place where I saw.
I see a reed with a broken stem in the field
that is holding his neck in peril.
It resembled a buried rebellion
and those unfinished revolutions
that had taken place in me.
The revolution turned the swamp into a cesspool.
I saw a rotted tree from the top of head.
The tree could not have gone through the winter.
Someday it will become a wilderness here too.
Even if I call a name,
there will be no twigs to answer the wind blowing over its
body. No pure man can be found on the dust,
and in the distant future,
himself who does not know
who he was will return here.
Who I was,
I will wait for the answer from the person
who decided to come.

Those people who knew me,
those myriad pieces that are falling down here,
when the puzzle aligned,
so imperceptibly, spring will come.
Ask me if I can get back the image
I lost in the beginning of time,
and when the season returns,
the density of the air in the east
and the dazzling sensation in the dawn fog,
I'll sing a song together
and say goodbye to me
that I've forgotten in that time,

May

I do not want to be parasitic again
in that season.
Friends!
That afternoon hundreds of rose flowers
fell in the square,
and I made a pledge not to boast of the glorious days of
youth again in this season.
They were not there,
and could not see the men
who had fallen down with the grass on the road,
nor the owl who had not been sleeping
in the middle of the night,
in the back of the village,
in keeping there.
So we had a sleepless night.
I saw the back of a camel falling down
with souls and thirst that I could not meet.
Cut the day off from the calendar
and place a candle on an altar
where no one can reach,
I saw the back of those who prostrated
with sorrow and dry branches
that could not make green leaves
despite the heavy rain of the season.
The birds of May who sat on the branches of the tree and

told us all about the day were no longer there.
We cannot remember the face of mothers
who turned and cried before the dead
for a while now.
It was a series of days
that I could not remember again.
Youth has not been seen all day in a fog
that never disappears the shortcut to the deep season,
where there is no shade of trees anywhere,
is no longer parasitic.
If the fallen petals
are not in the shade of a tree
that they cannot rest comfortably,

wind

If you do not stand in the middle of it,
you will not know. You cannot hear their stories
unless you are at the center of an indifferent density that
comes from somewhere you cannot touch
and stays for a while.
There I see a soul of a miscarried woman
clutching famished.
Perhaps her story, which is not audible,
flows out of reach.
Screaming is heard in the dry forest.
The ancient glacier remained a mark on the rocks.
It was a gesture that hastened the last.
Knowing it beforehand,
the ungrown children on the hill were flying kites.
They were looking up a sunset hill with
the string of a kite that might break when.
Knowing everything, they were there.
So beautiful and strong,
they stood in the center
and talked to the old stories from afar.
Soul galaxies floating in space,
the depth of which was unknown.
I would like to find an ancient temple buried
in the sand of envoys
where I cannot still hear from them.

All I can hear is the sound of camels lost in the desert.

Rainy season

The mother who lost the baby was crying,
wearing a long skirt made of hemp.
I have heard the story of a mountain village
that no one has ever been to.
I did not see the sun in the summer of that year.
Children were swept by the water in the valley has risen
due to the heavy rain
and reached to the village,
and there they hung on the branches,
and were waving in the wind,
with their swollen feet sticking out
as they were longing for sunlight.
The souls of the lost children were thundering.
The railing of the bridge,
which was broken by heavy rain,
was not seen at the end.
No one waited for the railroad to reach Seoul.
The lines of memory, lingering feelings of not being able to
connect to anything, had to be discarded.
These marks will not be erased.
a day when the thick layers of curtains are lifted
to shine upon the traces of visitors on the ground,
when tears are stopped
and even wounds look beautiful;
I look at the flock of birds flying up the hill in the east.

They became crying there.
Sometimes, it is the only thing that scared so many persons.
They became us there and here.

old tree

You see the old trees of the often-visited forest,
the vines that grew up with the trunk of the tree
that our forefathers had seen together,
the strength of what they thought so deep and so long,
that the wind of the forest could not overcome.
There is another cry to hear,
it was a longing for a new world and a sign of areas to keep.
Whichever path you choose,
do not be tired on that way.
You will not feel hunger anymore
in this empty space
that you have come to this place,
you are my true friend and saint of deep thought.
We must send our sacred offerings to the desert,
so let us see the humility and the strong faith
that we have to fill the space with our earnest wishes.
Never forget this place there
and send to the wanders on the dust your words
that wrote it down on the petals
that are lighter than the grass.
In this empty space,
which will be filled again even if it is empty,
I will always wait for a rich table.

serenade

This sorrow was not always tamed.
They had to listen to the drunken man's song outside the
broken window every night
because of the careless visitor's mockery
and their usual veiled conscience.
There were many nights of pain.
In the square, where our consciousness is buried,
in the dark, the requiem for some of us that never end.
I always had to watch the full moon of April
on the spot.
It was probably because of the song
that lasted until late at night
that I could not miss even in the old,
faded photo album.
On a day of thawing consciousness and sensations,
on a long night that was short,
reminiscing over the colorful stage,
we should listen to a girl's tune.
Was she there?
Unshakable disillusionment
has often led to illusion.
The man, who was not the shy being,
kept his spot, constantly questioning the sound
and even giving himself up.
Now we have to wake up from our conscious night.

There is nowhere to go back,
but we need to stay awake
and have a new day with the souls who left.
The song to be sung for the day will be circulating somewhere,
and after this night,
I will listen again, my man! My songs!

Arounding the border

If you look at water strider on the surface,
you have a vague idea of
how exciting it is to walk around the border.
When you look at the wonder of the unbreakable things,
the stubbornness under the moon light,
you look like the person you have wanted
to see so much.
When an unknown wind from the boundary blows,
an old face shuddered and buried
beneath the deep water rises.
I could not remember that day.
Everything was disappearing below the surface,
and the tremors that shook this place did not know
it was a little sobbing back then.
The time to wait until midnight has always been fear.
My obsession with everything
that was sinking made my legs
and arms stiff
and persons no longer looked for me.
There, I saw a girl becoming a plaster.
Strong buoyancy began to grow on the hard flesh.
The warriors who always live
with their dreams of immortality,
this empty gesture,
which seemed to catch the wind in a time

as fleeting as the Milky Way,
floating in the night sky,
where I cannot look back.

placard

The cries of the vagabonds
were heard on the garbage dumps,
which were not purged until the night of
disgust and nausea.
Their doodles and the mockery of
the unconscionable white classes,
anyone who takes away these turbulent products,
could have reached dawn.
In a country where flowers do not bloom,
when you call it by its name,
there are no living creatures here that can breathe.
Can you hear this cry,
a place full of cold cadavers under pressure?
When did you remember our beings?
Graffiti is another sanctuary,
where dream children grow up.
On the day these curtains are lifted up,
our revolution will begin,
and you will remember the names of those who
remain here that night.
Those who took the subway past midnight,
those wandering underground,
no one knew but me that they were warriors.
It was not the body that was shaking;
it was my spirit that was becoming impoverished.
On the day when the dream of revolution disappeared,

there were only the advertisements of
the decadent tavern,
the prostitutes of the poor in the soul,
and the traces of the cats in the street.
All I hear is that you have to leave here
without hesitation,
but the rotten spirits that are tied up are
shaking and crying on the ground.

{Books of Y.J.J.Han}

Novels:

Refugees, Ali
Hastings Street
Swine Fever

Collections of Poem:

The Old Memories of Tynehead
Space
Refugees
The Qs about Aiists
Epistles from the drifters
Wetland City
Gastown

swine fever

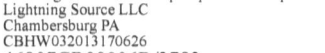